DANGEROUS MAGIC

DONNA GRANT

DANGEROUS MAGIC

Copyright © 2012 Donna Grant

Excerpt from *A Dark Guardian* copyright © 2012 by Donna Grant
Cover artist: Croco Designs

ISBN: 0988208407
ISBN-13: 978-0-9882084-0-7

PRAISE FOR
DONNA GRANT

5! Top Pick! "An absolutely must read! From beginning to end, it's an incredible ride."—*Night Owl Romance*

5 Hearts! "I definitely recommend *Dangerous Highlander*, even to skeptics of paranormal romance – you just may fall in love with the MacLeods."—*The Romance Reader*

5 Tombstones! "Another fantastic series that melds the paranormal with the historical life of the Scottish highlander in this arousing and exciting adventure. The men of MacLeod castle are a delicious combination of devoted brother, loyal highlander Lord and demonic God that ooze sex appeal and inspire some very erotic daydreams as they face their faults and accept their fate."—*Bitten By Books*

4 Stars! "Grant creates a vivid picture of Britain centuries after the Celts and Druids tried to expel the Romans, deftly merging magic and history. The result is a wonderfully dark, delightfully well-written tale. Readers will eagerly await the next Dark Sword book." —*Romantic Times BOOKreviews*

"Donna Grant spins a searing and intense tale [that] will keep readers spellbound." —*Romance Reviews Today*

"Highly enjoyable and super sexy."—*The Book Lush*

"Donna Grant's Dark Sword series is slowly climbing to my top three. LOVE IT!" —*Good Choice Reading*

THE WICKED TREASURE SERIES
Seized by Passion
Enticed by Ecstasy
Captured by Desire

DRUIDS GLEN SERIES
Highland Mist
Highland Nights
Highland Dawn
Highland Fires
Highland Magic
Dragonfyre

STAND ALONE BOOKS
Savage Moon
Mutual Desire
Forever Mine

ANTHOLOGIES
The Pleasure of His Bed
The Mammoth Book of Scottish Romance

Chapter One

Forest near Wolfglynn Castle
Summer, 1128

The darkness pulled at his soul, demanding release, yearning to ravage the land in blood and death. Every day it became harder and harder to fight it, to remember the man he used to be.

But then again, he'd known the outcome of his battle from the first moment the darkness had seeped into him.

Cade paused in sharpening his sword and looked over the turbulent sea to observe the small rowboat as it neared Wolfglynn Castle. Every morning, he watched the boat bring the beautiful, vibrant Francesca to the castle, her fiery hair drawing his gaze like a beacon. And every evening, he watched her return to the small isle across the sea.

It had become a ritual, just like honing his weapons and stalking the forest for an enemy he knew would strike soon—very soon.

Cade's gaze jerked away from Francesca as something stirred in the trees. He stood, sword at the ready, and walked silently toward the sound, listening for warnings that it might be *him*.

"Cade?"

He stopped and sighed.

"Cade. Please," Drogan called from where he stood at the edge of the foliage. "Just talk to me."

But Cade didn't dare. It was painful enough being so near a man he'd called brother, but Cade was willing to bear the torture in an effort to save Drogan's life. It was only because of Drogan that Cade didn't go hunting Nigel himself.

Baron Nigel Creely. Cade's lip curled in a sneer at the mere thought of him. The bastard had turned Cade into what he was, the same man who had already tried to kill Drogan once.

Drogan had won the first battle, but Nigel hadn't given up. Cade knew all too well that once Nigel wanted someone dead, he would stop at nothing to see it done. Which was why Cade hid in the forest.

"Cade. I know you're out there." Drogan sighed and ran a hand through his long auburn hair. "What do I need to say to get you to come inside the castle?"

There's nothing you can say, brother.

The darkness had nearly claimed Drogan, but he'd managed to fight it, and with his woman by his side, Drogan had beaten it once and for all. Cade didn't want to put the darkness near Drogan again, not when it was so much a part of Cade that there was no separating the two anymore.

He moved as close to Drogan as he dared before he stopped and watched his friend. Cade still remembered being told he was transferred to the king's private guard. Cade had been young, so very young, but his talent with a blade had brought him to Gerard and Drogan—two of the finest swordsmen in all of England.

The two were a handful of years older than Cade, but they had quickly formed a brotherhood. Cade had eagerly learned everything the men had taught him, and each month, his skill continued to grow.

Which was what caught Nigel's attention. If only Cade had known then what he knew now, he would never have allowed Nigel to sink his claws into him.

Drogan shifted from one foot to the other, his hand on the pommel of his sword as his gaze scanned the trees. "You know you are welcome anytime, Cade. I'd like to introduce you to my son. Serena wants to get to know you as well. And I just want to sit across from you and share a meal as we used to."

Cade closed his eyes. He knew he shouldn't listen to Drogan. It was too easy to let his friend's words affect him. Drogan thought he knew everything about him, but Drogan knew nothing. If he had an inkling as to what Cade had done since that fateful night so many years ago when their brotherhood had broken, Drogan wouldn't invite him into his castle.

"I won't give up on you," Drogan murmured before he turned on his heel and strode toward the castle.

Cade leaned back against a tree and sighed. God, how he missed talking to Drogan and Gerard. When he had learned of Nigel's plans to kill both men, Cade hadn't hesitated to ensure his friends' survival.

Gerard and his family were once more at their castle, and though the threat of Nigel would never go away, for some reason Nigel wanted Drogan before Gerard. Most likely it was because Drogan had led their brotherhood. Drogan had been the strongest of them, the best of them.

While Cade had been the weakest, the worst.

His gaze snapped open when he smelled lilacs and felt the tingle of magic along his skin. He whirled around to find the witch, Francesca, standing twenty paces from him.

Many times he'd followed her in the forest while she picked herbs, though he had never spoken to her. His gaze drank in the sight of her exquisite beauty, from the dark red tresses that hung in a thick braid over her shoulder to her creamy skin, unblemished and pure.

Tawny eyes stared at him under gently arched brows. Her lips were curved at the corners, as if she knew some secret he did not. Her gown of yellow hugged her breasts, and the decorative, painted belt that wound about her waist and hips only brought more attention to her delicious curves.

Cade's balls tightened in response. Since the first time he had seen her over a year ago, he hadn't been able to squelch the lust that pounded through him each time he looked at her.

"Will you never talk to him, my lord?"

Her voice was soft, rich and seductive. He fought the urge to run, to disappear into the trees as he always did when someone got too close to him. Yet he hadn't spoken to anyone in...months. And she was here. Asking him a question.

"Don't call me 'my lord.'" His voice sounded harsh and rusty.

Her head tilted to the side. "Are you not a titled lord? Do you not have land and a castle of your own?"

Cade cursed inwardly. Drogan must have spoken about him. "You shouldn't be alone out here."

"You're protecting me. As you always are."

When he furrowed his brow, she smiled.

"I may not acknowledge you, but I always feel you when I'm in the forest. You follow me, don't you? Protecting me?"

Cade stretched his shoulders. "If Drogan won't supply a guard, someone has to watch over you."

"I don't need a guard."

He could argue with her on that point, but decided against it. Her strength of will was obvious, and not just because she was a witch, or a *bana-bhuidseach*, as she called herself. She wasn't the only witch at Wolfglynn, though. Drogan's wife, Serena, was also a witch.

"You aren't going to tell me why you won't talk to Drogan, are you?" Francesca asked.

Cade shook his head. "There's nothing to tell."

"Then tell me this, warrior. Why do you stay in the forest?"

Cade opened his mouth to speak, but she continued on.

"Could it be because you know Nigel will return? I would think that you were on Nigel's side except for the pain I see on your face every time Drogan asks you to come to the castle."

Cade swallowed and took a step away from her. Francesca always unsettled him. Maybe it was the way her tawny eyes regarded him, as if she saw through to his black soul. Maybe it was her beauty. Or maybe it was because when she was near, her magic clashed against his darkness, prickling his skin with...something unnamable.

One brow lifted. "Do you fear me, Cade?"

He feared what he might do to her, but he wasn't going to tell her that. "It's unwise for you to be so near me."

Her gaze softened. "It's the darkness, isn't it? That's how I always know when you are near. I feel it."

"My apologies."

"There's no need to apologize. I know that as long as you are near, I'm safe."

He hadn't expected her to say that—nor did he expect the little thrill those words caused him.

She let out a deep breath. "Everyone needs a friend. Even you. We all know Nigel will return, so there's no use in thinking you must fight him yourself."

"I won't let him get near Drogan and his family." *Or you.*

"Let us help you then."

He shook his head. "You felt the darkness in Drogan. His is nothing compared to mine."

"I know," she whispered.

"You risk too much by being near me, witch."

For long moments, she held his gaze. "It's tearing Drogan apart that you're out here alone. And if I had to gamble on it, I would say you feel as much pain, or more, than he does."

Cade took another step away from her. Drogan might have spoken of him, but Cade knew him well enough to be sure that Drogan had kept much more private. Which was how it should be. No one needed to know of their deeds, especially not the beautiful, alluring witch standing in front of him.

She thought him good despite the darkness surrounding him. He wanted her to continue to think him a decent person for as long as she could. All too soon, she would realize just what a monster he was.

Pheasants startled and flew into the air. As soon as Francesca turned her head, Cade slid behind a tree. She didn't seem the least bit surprised to find him gone, though her gaze did search for him just as Drogan's had.

Cade drank in her ethereal beauty until she turned and headed back to the castle. He ran a hand down his face and sagged against the tree. He had never expected to talk to her, much less that she would seek him out.

Already he missed the tingling of his skin that vanished with her. Once she was safely in the castle, he walked to where she had stood. He inhaled deeply and caught the soft scent of lilacs.

Chapter Two

Francesca didn't want to leave the forest. She'd finally given in to the urge to seek out Cade, and she had been lucky enough to stumble upon him.

She clasped her shaking hands together and paused outside the castle walls. The pain etched on his face as he listed to Drogan had made her heart catch. His loneliness was palpable, but he wouldn't let anyone near enough to befriend him.

Not even Drogan, who claimed they had been closer than brothers.

She'd heard bits and pieces of the past that had broken their group apart, but Francesca had a feeling there was much more to it, more than even Drogan knew.

Unable to stop herself, she looked over her shoulder at the trees. She could feel Cade's gaze on her. She had wanted to get closer to him, to look into the vivid blue of his eyes, but the darkness that surrounded him pushed her away. Or maybe that was Cade.

She stepped into the castle and instantly missed his gaze. She licked her lips and made her feet continue on to the great hall. There she found Serena sitting at the dais with her son on her lap.

"Good morn," Serena said brightly.

Francesca forced a smile and slid into the seat beside her fellow *bana-bhuidseach*.

"Drogan said a storm was coming in," Serena said.

Francesca nodded. "Aye. I'll have to leave earlier today to reach the isle before it hits."

She watched Serena feeding her son for a time as her thoughts turned once more to Cade. After Nigel had attacked the first time, Francesca had returned to Wolfglynn each day to strengthen the castle with magic.

"The castle is as prepared as it can get," Serena murmured before she raised her gaze to look at Francesca. "I enjoy your company, especially after thinking I was the last *bana-bhuidseach* left, but tell me the real reason you continue to return."

Francesca couldn't hold Serena's gaze. She looked away and remembered the vibrant blue of Cade's eyes. There was so much she wanted to tell Serena, but she couldn't. No one could know. No one.

"Francesca?"

She shrugged. "I like to be prepared."

Serena snorted. "You're lying, and I don't need magic to know that."

"Is the chamber ready?" she asked to change the subject.

Serena narrowed her gaze before she nodded. "Drogan said it would be finished today."

Francesca ran her hand over the smooth wood of the table. The chamber had been her idea—a place protected by magic, a place where Serena and her son could stay when Nigel attacked again.

"Is he coming?"

Francesca jerked her eyes to Serena, knowing she spoke of Nigel. "He is, but I can't pinpoint a day."

"We've waited over a year."

"And in that time, he has grown stronger. Let's not forget he attacked Grayson as well."

"You knew he would."

It wasn't a question. Francesca sighed. "I warned Grayson to be careful. I knew he would be able to take care of himself."

She just hadn't seen he was also a *bana-bhuidseach*. It had been many decades since their kind had produced a male witch.

"He wants to help us," Serena said as she turned her son towards her and patted his back.

Francesca let the baby wrap his small fist around her finger. "Grayson will only put himself and Adrianna in danger."

"I know, but I would love for you to meet her. Can you imagine the three of us together?"

Francesca smiled as she imagined the three female witches in the same castle. "It would be wonderful."

"I've beat the curse, Fran. So has Adrianna. There is still hope for you."

Nay, not an ounce. "Of course there is. Once this Nigel business is over, I can look to the future."

"I've seen several of the men watching you. You could have your pick of them."

Francesca placed her hand atop Serena's before she rose to her feet. "I look forward to it."

The baby began to fuss, giving Francesca the time she needed to exit the hall before Serena could say more. She was thrilled that Serena had broken the curse of their people, but Francesca knew she herself wouldn't be so lucky.

She shut the castle door behind her and stood atop the steps, letting her eyes scan the bailey and battlements until she found Drogan. She lifted her skirts and hurried down the steps and across the bailey to the stairs that led to the battlements.

Francesca paused once she reached the top. Drogan stood staring at the forest, and she didn't need her magic to know he thought of Cade.

"There is nothing you can say that will lure him inside these walls."

Drogan looked over his shoulder at her, his golden eyes clashing with hers. There was pain in his depths, but also determination and drive. "There has to be something."

Francesca moved to stand beside him. "It's because he cares about you and your new family that he doesn't come."

"How do you know this?" Drogan's voice had taken on a hard edge, and his gaze narrowed as he watched her.

"I spoke with him after you left the forest."

Drogan eyes closed for a moment before he faced her. "As far as I know, he hasn't spoken to anyone since the day Nigel attacked last year."

"I got lucky, I suppose."

"Please. Tell me what he said."

She glanced at the trees, wondering if Cade watched them. "He waits in the woods for Nigel. He plans to attack Nigel before Nigel can attack you."

"As good as Cade is, he won't stand a chance against that bastard alone. I need to get him to the castle."

She shook her head. "Whenever you go into the forest, he is always near. Watching you. Listening as you talk to him."

"Why doesn't he speak to me?"

She wished she knew the answer. "I don't know. It causes him great pain, though. He wants to talk to you, but it's as if he doesn't allow himself."

Drogan ran a hand down his face. "He and Gerard were the brothers I never had. It was my job to look after Cade, since he was the youngest. I failed him, Francesca."

"I don't know whether you did or not, and that doesn't seem to matter to Cade. He has secluded himself in the forest to protect you."

Drogan faced the wall and leaned his hands on the stones. "If only I had done things differently. Our lives changed forever in the space of a heartbeat. I wish I knew what Nigel said to Cade to make him turn away from us."

Francesca turned toward the trees and let the breeze from the sea surround her. The urge to return to the forest and seek out Cade was strong. She could feel the darkness that surrounded him even now.

"He won't win against the darkness, will he?" Drogan asked.

"It depends on if he wants to win."

Drogan dropped his head. "We need to make him want to win against it. If I could, so can he. I cannot lose him, Francesca. I cannot lose him."

She stayed as she was for long moments after Drogan left. There was nothing more for her to do at Wolfglynn. Every stone, every weapon had been filled with magic to withstand an attack by Nigel. Yet she knew it wouldn't be enough. It would never be enough.

There was only one thing that could destroy Nigel. She just hoped no innocents were taken down with him.

Francesca closed her eyes and smiled. Cade was watching her just as he did every morning and every evening. She wasn't sure when she had come to look forward to that feeling of warmth, but now she couldn't go a day without it. She had faced brutal storms and harsh winter weather just to have his gaze on her.

It was a dangerous game she played, but one she couldn't seem to shy away from.

Cade guarded Wolfglynn and her people day and night. No one ever saw him unless he wanted to be seen, which was never. She wasn't sure how she had managed to come upon him that morning.

Her fingers dug into the stones as she recalled his golden locks that hung to his shoulders in thick waves. His skin was darkened by the sun, making his blue eyes shine brightly. She longed to run her fingers along his square jaw and chin to his wide mouth.

He was tall and broad shouldered, which made his light brown tunic and jerkin mold to his muscular chest and arms. His dark breeches were snug against his powerfully built legs. He was an amazing specimen, but it wasn't him or the darkness that surrounded him that gave her pause. It was his weapons.

A large, curved dagger was strapped to his hip, with another smaller dirk tucked into the top of his right boot. On his back, crisscrossing scabbards held duel swords unlike anything she'd ever seen.

The handles were nearly white, showing the smooth lines of ash wood, and adorned with silver guards and pommels. The blades weren't as long as most swords and curved ever so slightly, but the way he held the knives, it was obvious he knew how to wield them with deadly quick precision.

She took in a deep breath and stilled as she saw movement in the forest. Her heart beat faster, and she thought of going to him. Would he allow her to find him again? Would he talk to her?

Francesca made herself turn away from the trees. She would only hurt Cade more if she couldn't fight the desire to be near him. But, oh, the feel of excitement that rushed through her when she'd come upon him.

She had been afraid to move, afraid to speak for fear that he would disappear. And he had, but not before answering her questions. He had been as surprised as she was at finding him, and the roughness of his voice told her that he hadn't spoken in a very long time.

Chills raced along her spine. He watched her still.

And she loved it.

You can't.

But if only she could....

Chapter Three

Cade couldn't seem to help himself. His gaze sought Francesca whether he wanted it to or not. He found himself contemplating what she and Drogan spoke about atop the battlements. Could it have been him?

He wondered what the witch thought of him. Had he frightened her? She hadn't appeared scared, but then again, she hadn't gotten close to him.

Cade needed to patrol the forest, but he couldn't tear his gaze from Francesca. As soon as she had entered the castle, he had scanned the battlements, hoping for a glimpse of her.

Her courage surprised him. Most who entered the forest cast nervous glances around in the hopes of not seeing him. But not the witch. She had sought him out. Yet, just as with Drogan, he couldn't allow himself to speak with her again. Too much was at stake for him to ruin it because her beauty and grace called to him as nothing had before.

When she walked from the battlements, disappearing from his view, he made himself turn and patrol the forest as he did many times each day. Even as he did, his mind wandered to Francesca. She hadn't seemed uneasy in speaking to him—it was almost as if the darkness hadn't affected her.

His steps slow and measured, he looked at the ground, the trees, and the sky for any signs that Nigel had arrived. Nigel was a crafty arse. He would send spies ahead of him to scope Wolfglynn before he attacked.

Cade had been ready for the assault for months. He was itching for a fight, but more than that, he wanted to battle Nigel before the darkness took him completely.

He paused and knelt to study a track in the dirt. It was a wolf, but larger than the pack that had the run of Wolfglynn. Prickles of apprehension stole down his spine. Cade needed to find the wolf quickly.

Cade straightened and followed the tracks for hours. The pawprints circled the castle several times. In a few places, he found the tracks deeper where the wolf had paused and stared at the castle.

Anger ripped through Cade, making the darkness roar to be free. He fisted his hands and tamped down the evil that resided in him. He was angry at himself for not learning of the wolf earlier, but if he wasn't careful, the darkness would take hold of him, and everything he sought to protect he would kill.

Cade took in several steadying breaths before he turned once more to the tracks. They disappeared as suddenly as they appeared, and they were fresh. Very fresh. Which meant the wolf was still in the forest.

Wolfglynn had water to her back and rolling hills that gave way to the forest. The woodland itself was thicker on the right side of the castle. And it was large, extending well past the boundaries of Drogan's land.

Cade continued through the trees, searching for more tracks. Wolfglynn had a pack of wolves. The castle always had, which was where it got its name. In all the years, no one had been attacked by the wolves, and no one was allowed to hunt them. Drogan's people let the occasional sheep kill go, and they were compensated by Drogan when they did.

Over the decades, however, the pack had grown smaller and smaller until Cade feared there would be no more wolves in England. His gaze spotted one of the larger tracks at the same time he heard the laughter of children.

"Shite," he murmured as he started for the youngsters.

His legs pumped faster, and his strides grew longer. The trees flew by him in a whoosh. His only thought was getting to the children in time, because he had no doubt the wolf he tracked had been sent from Nigel.

The thought of the children dying pushed him even faster. He spotted the group of kids just inside the forest, their laughter ringing in his ears. He was nearly there. He was going to reach them before the wolf.

And then he spotted something off to his left.

Cade glanced and saw the large black wolf. He reached back and withdrew his blades as he began to yell at the children. A woman was with them. She looked up and let out a scream as she spotted the wolf.

Cade's lungs burned, but he dared not slow, for if he did, that would mean the death of the children. He couldn't have that added to his conscious.

What is one more death?

He tamped down the darkness that urged him to give into the evil.

"Nay," he bellowed as he launched himself atop the wolf just before the beast jumped on the children.

Cade landed hard and rolled to his feet. He faced the wolf, which stood growling at him, its long fangs dripping with saliva.

"You won't kill them," he said to the wolf.

The wolf's lips peeled back as he growled and hunched low.

Cade grinned. It was a fight he had been hungering for. The fight would feed the darkness, but it would also lessen its hold on him for a few days.

He swung his knives in front of him. "You want to sink your teeth into something? Try me."

The fur on the back of the wolf's shoulder rose. It was a big animal, nearly twice the size of the other wolves on Wolfglynn land. But Cade knew who had sent it. He knew what drove it.

The wolf leapt at him. Cade lifted his knives and raked them under the animal's belly, simultaneously ducking to avoid the wolf's claws. Cade whirled around and saw the animal limping before he let out a snarl. This time, when the wolf attacked, he leapt for Cade's face.

Cade spun to the side, but not before the wolf's claws scraped down his back. Cade hissed and slung his arm back. He smiled when his blade sunk into the fur and the animal let out a yelp of pain.

The wolf released him and hobbled to the side. Cade focused on the pain of his wounds instead of the darkness that demanded he give in to the need to kill. Only once before had he ever given in, and the act still haunted his dreams.

The animal was badly injured, but he would continue to fight until he was dead. Cade took a step toward the wolf, but the beast turned its gaze to the children. Cade made the mistake of looking at the group. The children huddled around the woman, all of them staring in horror. But it was the fiery-haired beauty behind them who caught Cade's attention.

The wind had begun to pick up, and the sky darkened with the storm that had been brewing over the water for days. He turned his back to Francesca and focused on the wolf. Cade twisted his blades in unison and took a step toward the animal.

The wolf growled and lunged at him. Cade leaned to the side while the beast's teeth missed his leg by breaths. Cade stood his ground and waited, impatient to kill the animal. The wolf lunged again, and this time, his teeth sunk into Cade's thigh.

Cade let out a bellow and plunged both knives into the wolf. The wolf instantly released him, throwing back its head and howling in pain. Cade pulled his weapons out and staggered backward.

He expected the wolf to attack again, but when Cade looked up, the black wolf was surrounded by Wolfglynn's pack. Their growls at the wounded intruder let him know the black wolf wouldn't live for very much longer. Cade turned to the group behind him.

"Get them to the castle," he bellowed at Francesca and the other woman.

Cade spotted Drogan and his men riding hard toward the forest. Cade slipped behind a group of trees and made sure Drogan was occupied with getting the children to safety.

The growls, barks and yelps of pain from the black wolf consumed the forest as the pack attacked. Blood ran down Cade's leg in thick rivulets, and his back ached. He would have to see to the wounds before he could resume his patrol of the forest. Because Nigel never sent just one.

Cade cleaned off his knives and returned them to their scabbards before he started to make his way to the sea. There was a cave he used to store supplies. It also came in handy when the weather grew too harsh.

He was halfway to the cave when he felt the prickle on his skin.

Francesca.

He stopped and turned to face her. "You shouldn't be here."

"You're injured. I can help."

Cade shook his head. "You need to return to the castle. It's not safe in the forest."

"The wolf is dead. Please. Let me tend to your wounds, and then I will leave."

He opened his mouth to respond when he heard a horse. Cade grasped Francesca's hand and pulled her toward him where he flattened her against a tree.

Lust burned his blood at the feel of her soft body against him. One of her hands gripped his shoulder while the other rested over his heart. It had been so long since he had held a woman in his arms. Even the times he sought out a woman to relieve his body, he always took her from behind so she faced away from him.

Yet now, the one woman who mesmerized him was in his arms, his face inches from hers. The pulse at her neck beat wildly as she lifted her tawny gaze to his.

"Ca—"

He put his hand over her mouth to stop her words. Whoever was in the forest wasn't friendly, and Cade refused to let anything happen to her.

Her breath fanned the back of his hand. Unable to stop the desire pumping through him, Cade moved his hand until only his thumb rested against her plump lips. The need to kiss her, to taste her, was...overwhelming and painful. He couldn't remember the last time he had kissed a woman, and he wasn't sure he knew how anymore.

His thumb caressed her bottom lip, causing his balls to tighten and blood to pound in his ears. He wanted her with a ferocity that rivaled the need to kill Nigel.

Lightning streaked across the sky seconds before thunder boomed. Cade's breath caught in his throat when Francesca's fingers gripped him. He needed to get her to the castle and out of the storm, but he couldn't make his body move. Now that he felt her soft curves, he never wanted to let her go.

Kiss her. Just one taste, just one touch.

It was all he wanted. Just one taste. His head lowered until their lips were nearly brushing. Her magic washed over him, making his skin quiver and his heart quicken. And then he realized that if her magic could affect him, his darkness could affect her.

Cade jerked out of arms.

Her brow furrowed. "Cade?"

"Come," he said and took her hand as he raced toward the cave.

They had gotten just a few steps when the sky opened and the rain fell in such thick sheets that he couldn't see where he was headed. He knew the path well enough to make it blindfolded, but he slowed because of the rocks and Francesca's skirt.

By the time they made it into the cave, both were drenched. Cade set about starting a fire from the stack of wood he kept in the cave. There was enough wood to last for three days, but he knew he wouldn't last three heartbeats being so near Francesca.

"The storm rolled in quicker than expected," she said.

He glanced up from the fire to see her standing in the entrance, her arms wrapped about herself. She shivered slightly in the sea breeze.

Cade rose to his feet and retrieved one of the blankets. He walked to her and held the blanket out. "There are more if you need them."

She looked from the blanket to his face. "And you?"

"I'll be fine."

"I need to see to your injuries."

He shrugged. "You need to get out of your wet clothes before you catch a chill. Drogan and Phineas will have my head."

"Drogan's uncle knows I can take care of myself."

Cade had no doubt, but he said nothing. Finally, she took the blanket and walked toward the back of the cave. It took everything Cade had to turn his back to her instead of watching her, or helping her, remove her wet gown.

He inhaled through his mouth and concentrated on breathing instead of pulling her into his arms and kissing her, touching her...tasting her. By God, he had never known anything so torturous as to have the one thing he wanted above all else near to him, yet not be able to have her.

If only he had said no to Nigel. If only he had found a way to freedom, he might have been able to pull Francesca into his arms and not worry about the darkness affecting her. If only he could battle the darkness as Drogan and Gerard did, then maybe he could have a taste of happiness.

You don't deserve happiness.

And God forgive him, it was the truth. Nigel wasn't the only one who needed to die. He did as well.

Cade heard the rustle of material as Francesca removed her gown. He fisted his hands and stared unseeing into the rain, imagining her body bared to him. Her lips turned up in a smile as her arms rose to welcome him.

He pictured her body, warm and willing and open to him. She would be wet, her arousal filling his senses. He would slide into her heat, thrusting into her soft body until she screamed his name as she peaked.

Cade's body was covered in sweat just thinking about Francesca. He shook with the effort to keep looking to the sea, to not touch her. But what if she came to him? What if she tried to touch him? It would be too much. He was on the edge already, and she would send him over.

"*Yes, yes. Yes!*" the darkness clamored. "*Let her loosen us.*"

Nay, Cade screamed inside his head.

He smelled lilacs and knew she had drawn closer to him. He yearned for her touch like the ground craved water. But he could not give in. For her sake as well as his.

"There's food and water for you."

"Cade?"

She was so near. All he had to do was turn around, and he would find her. He had already given in and touched her lips, but he dared not do more. One more touch would snap his control, and the fact she wore nothing but a blanket now made his lust surge through him, made his blood pound in his ears.

"I'll return later," he said and stepped into the rain before he could wrap his arms around her.

Chapter Four

Francesca watched Cade disappear into the storm. The lightning continued to flash across the sky, and she knew he had left his only shelter because of her.

And she hadn't tended his wounds.

She tugged the blanket tighter around her. Unable to stop shaking, she made her way to the fire and sat near it, letting the flames warm her.

Cade had said there was food, but that wasn't what she hungered for. She wanted Cade. She knew she courted disaster, but she couldn't help herself. He was strength and courage and heroic fighting against an evil that wanted to devour him.

He was a warrior.

The darkness that surrounded him had been evident while he battled the black wolf, but he had held it in check. It wasn't until he had touched her lips and brought her to the cave that she had seen him waver against the darkness.

Her reaction to his body surprised her. Her nipples ached, and the fluttering in her stomach had yet to go away. Her breasts had swollen the moment his body pressed against hers. His hand on her mouth had been feather light, and when his thumb had moved over her lip, the caress had sent chills racing over her heated skin.

All thoughts of the wolf and the weather had vanished when she looked into his vibrant blue eyes. He had nearly kissed her. Her breath had locked in her lungs as she silently begged him to touch his mouth to hers.

She had seen Drogan and Serena kiss. There was passion and desire in a kiss, but it could be so much more. And she wanted Cade to be the man who kissed her, the man who made her feel as a woman should.

Francesca tucked her legs against her chest and rested her chin atop her knees. With the blanket wrapped around her and the fire blazing, warmth soon cocooned her. Her mind was never far from Cade, though. Seeing how he wielded his weapons let her know that Drogan hadn't exaggerated when he'd said Cade was the best he had ever seen. Cade had shown no fear in battling the wolf. In fact, he'd seemed to enjoy it.

She shivered as she imagined what would have happened had Cade not been there to stop the black wolf. His blades had whipped through the air as if they were an extension of his arms. And his eyes had glowed with a light that grew brighter as the battle went on.

Was that the darkness?

Francesca had been mesmerized watching him fight. Every step, every movement had lethal purpose. It was no wonder Nigel had wanted Cade as his own so desperately. Somehow, Nigel had gotten Cade, but at what cost? When had Cade stopped working for Nigel?

Some speculated Cade still had ties to Nigel, but Francesca doubted it. None of the dreams that gave her a glimpse into the future had shown her much about Cade. He was still a mystery, but a mystery she wanted to solve.

* * * * *

Cade hurried to the tree where he had nearly kissed Francesca. It was here he had heard the horse. Darkness pushed against his own, and he cursed low and long.

Nigel never sent just one.

The wolf was dead, but what awaited Cade now?

He unsheathed his knives and jerked his head to get the wet hair out of his eyes. Francesca's magic was gone, and he hated how he missed it, despised himself for needing it when he had distanced himself from everyone for so long. Just being close to her was enough for her magic to tamp down the darkness. It was selfish of him to stay near her. The saints only knew what his darkness was doing to her.

Cade moved from the tree, his feet silent as he stalked through the forest. The rain and thunder muffled any sound he might make, but it would do the same for his enemy.

His gaze constantly roamed around him, since he didn't want to be taken by surprise. At least with the storm everyone was inside, and Francesca was safe in the cave. Drogan would be taking care of his people and weathering the storm.

Cade heard the jingle of reins and knew the rider was near. He squinted through the rain to try and make out the horse but saw nothing. That didn't deter him, though. He halted beneath a low-hanging branch that blocked most of the rain. It was enough to give him the advantage over the hooded rider ahead of him to the left.

The rider nudged the horse forward until it was even with Cade. Cade shifted until he stood in front of the horse, his knives at the ready.

"I knew you would find me."

"Return to your master," Cade shouted over the rain.

The rider laughed. "Not before I finish what I've come to do."

"The wolf is dead, and you will be too if you don't leave now. Tell Nigel to come himself if he wants a battle."

"Oh, Nigel is on his way, Cade. Never fear."

Cade hated not knowing who the rider was, but with the hood of his cloak pulled forward, he couldn't see a face.

"You hate that you don't know who I am, don't you?" the rider asked, his voice low. "It doesn't really matter. We're all going to Hell eventually anyway."

"What did Nigel send you here to do?"

The rider's shifted in the saddle. "I've come to give a message to Drogan."

"And what message is that?"

"He'll understand once he finds his witch dead."

Anger ripped through Cade as the darkness begged him to give into the hate and rage. "Leave now. Or die."

"I could be a ploy, Cade. While you battle me, Nigel could slip into Wolfglynn and kill everyone."

"Why are you telling me this?"

The rider shrugged. "You got away from Nigel. I want to know how you did it."

Cade narrowed his gaze. "I walked away."

"Liar."

There was something familiar about the rider, something that kept nagging at Cade. "Why do you want to know?"

"Nigel...recruited...me in the same fashion as you. Let's just say, I could have gotten into the castle while you battled the wolf if I had really wanted to."

And it was the truth—Cade knew that. He wasn't sure if he could trust the rider, but with the battle approaching, Cade needed as many allies as he could find. Trusting the rider might be a mistake, but it was a chance Cade had to take.

"The leverage Nigel had over me didn't last. Once it was gone, so was I," Cade answered.

For several moments, the rider sat motionless. "Did Nigel kill your leverage?"

Cade lowered his weapons and mentally cringed when memories long buried surfaced. "Nay, Nigel didn't kill them."

"And he let you walk away."

"He didn't let me do anything. You're going to have to fight for your freedom, and be prepared to be hunted the rest of your life. Nigel doesn't let anything go. Does he have your soul?"

The rider gave a small jerk of his head. "He doesn't need permission anymore, Cade. He's grown much, much stronger. He can take any soul he wants."

"I don't believe that. He can't be that strong, not since last year when he was nearly defeated."

"He won't be coming alone this year. He wants you and Drogan dead. As well as the witches."

Plural. Which meant Nigel knew of Francesca. "How many witches does he think Drogan has?"

"He knows there are two here. He plans to make sure they die first."

Cade's heart clenched in fear. "Who are you?"

"A friend."

"I don't have any friends."

The rider cocked his head to the side. "And what are Drogan and Gerard? Enemies?"

"They were my friends. What I am—what we are—I cannot allow anyone to become familiar with me, because it would give Nigel more power. I refuse to ever be under his rule again."

The rain lessened, but the thunder and lightning continued behind him. He watched the rider for a moment before he asked once again, "Who are you?"

"Consider me a friend," he said and pulled back his cloak to reveal light brown hair and black eyes.

The breath left Cade in a whoosh. "Liam."

"Hello, Cade."

"Nigel told me you were dead."

Liam lifted one shoulder in a shrug, his face expressionless and his eyes emotionless. "I've been dead since I joined him."

"Does he have leverage against you?"

Liam nodded. "I thought I was the only one."

"I'm beginning to think that is how he recruits all his best fighters."

Liam shifted the reins in his hands. "I wasn't jesting about his power. Be prepared. Nigel will come at you sideways."

"Where are you going?" Now that Cade had found a friend, he didn't want Liam to leave.

"Away."

"And your...leverage?"

Liam dropped his gaze. "It was my wife. She hung herself when she saw what I had become."

Cade clenched his knives, his gut tightening for Liam. "I'm sorry."

"As am I. Nigel sent me to kill Drogan's witch, but I'll no longer do his bidding. Farewell," he said and turned his horse around.

"Be careful."

Liam raised his hand in response as he rode away.

Cade watched him, the rain taking Liam from sight sooner than Cade would have liked. Liam's visit had brought more questions than answers, and Cade found he wanted to talk further with Liam. Yet he knew Liam would provide no more information.

"Damn," Cade muttered.

He shifted and winced at the injury on his leg. He had forgotten it when the lust had taken hold of him; then he had needed to get away from Francesca, and then the talk with Liam. Now his leg and back throbbed. He wasn't ready to return to the cave, but he had to see to his wounds. He couldn't allow them to become infected. Not now, not when Nigel would arrive any day.

Cade blinked the water from his eyelashes and made his way back to the cave. He paused outside the entrance, unsure of being so near Francesca again. Already he could feel his skin tingle with her magic. He liked it. Maybe too much.

Droplets of rain ran down his back and trickled across the claw marks. He clenched his jaw at the pain and stepped into the cave.

His gaze found Francesca wrapped tightly in a blanket by the fire. Her chin rested on her knees as she stared into the flames. For long moments he watched her. Sometime while he had been gone, she had loosened her hear, and now the fiery strands dried in the firelight.

Suddenly, she lifted her head and looked at him. Their gazes collided, held. Cade wished he knew what she thought as she watched him. Did she see the evil that lurked beneath his skin? Did she sense the deeds he sought absolution for?

Did she see the man he had once been?

She rose to her feet in one fluid motion, the blanket held tight in her grip. "You left before I could look at your wounds."

Cade swallowed the flame of hope he felt whenever she was near and took a step towards her. He winced when his tunic brushed against the cuts on his back.

"You're in pain." Her voice held concern, which caused his gut to clench.

"The wounds are mild."

She snorted. "I wouldn't call the one on your leg mild. The wolf's teeth sunk deep."

Cade glanced at his leg. His breeches were torn where the wolf had grabbed hold of him and tugged, but it was the blood flowing down his leg and into his boot that made him sigh.

"Let me tend to your wounds."

He hesitated. Unsure why he had returned to her again, knowing that being near her caused him to feel...almost normal. He put her in danger every time he spoke to her.

"Please, Cade," she beseeched.

Chapter Five

Francesca held her breath as she waited for Cade to decide to let her help. She'd thought he wouldn't return. Her mind wondered at all sorts of things that could happen to him out in the storm, and then she had felt his gaze.

When she had turned to see him standing at the cave's entrance, his front blanketed in shadow, she'd had to fight the desire to rush to him.

Cade was like a wild animal. She would have to earn his trust slowly. If she earned it at all. It would be better for her if she walked away, forgot his arresting blue eyes and the way he made her heart accelerate and her blood heat.

She knew, but she couldn't do it.

For whatever reason, she was attracted to Cade. It was a hazardous path she had set them on, but she couldn't seem to stop herself. Never in her life had she been so lacking in self-control. Now, all she wanted to do was wrap her arms around him and hold her against him. The agony in his eyes frightened her much more than the darkness she saw mirrored in his soul.

She fisted her hands beneath the blanket and prayed he allowed her to help him in the only way she knew how.

"Did you find the food?" He moved to the fire, setting aside his twin knives and removing his jerkin.

Francesca tried not to eye the tears in the jerkin giving her a glimpse of his smooth chest as she shook her head. "I'm not hungry."

"The storm doesn't look to be letting up anytime soon."

She opened her mouth to answer when he pulled off his tunic, and she forgot to breath. His body rippled with muscles. His wide shoulders tapered to a narrow waist, where a trail of golden hair disappeared into the waist of his breeches. Several scars crisscrossed his chest, and one thick, jagged scar ran from his side around to his back.

He lowered himself to a rock and pulled off his boots before he withdrew the dagger and cut his breeches above the bite marks on his thigh.

Francesca licked her lips when he tore off the leg of his breeches and tossed them away. She knotted the blanket above her breasts and moved to her wet gown to tear off a piece of her skirt. Then she walked to the opening of the cave and rewet the material. She returned to Cade and knelt beside him, trying to ignore the way her stomach fluttered at being so near to him. She wiped away the blood on his leg.

"I wish we had dry bandages," she murmured.

"I'll be fine if you can stop the bleeding."

"I need my herbs to speed the healing." She made the mistake of looking up at him then. Though all *bana-bhuidseach* had some magic to heal, there were many, like her, who needed the aid of herbs to heal adequately.

His blue gaze burned her while the darkness surrounded both of them. Cade was dangerous. But then again, so was she.

She forced her gaze away from his and returned to his leg. His skin was warm, his leg dusted with golden hair and corded with muscles.

"The bite goes deep," she said as she leaned closer to the wound.

"He had long fangs."

She would've smiled had the situation not been so dire. "I've never seen that wolf before."

"It was sent by Nigel."

She paused in wiping the blood and glanced at Cade. "We need to tell Drogan."

"Drogan will know. He knows every wolf on his land."

"You went back to investigate the sound you heard before the storm, didn't you?"

He nodded.

She waited for him to tell her what happened. Long moments passed in silence until she got the leg wound to stop bleeding. When she moved to his back, he ripped his tunic in half and wrapped it around his leg.

The wounds on his back didn't go as deep as the bite marks, but they were long, marking almost all the way down his right side. She accepted a piece of his torn tunic and wet it in the rain before wiping away what little blood was left.

"These wounds have nearly stopped bleeding."

"Good."

She let out a breath. "Tell me what you found. Please."

His shoulders dropped. "Nigel never sends just one threat. They always come in pairs."

"So there was something out there?"

"Aye."

"What?"

"Not a what, but a who. His name is Liam."

"You know him?"

Cade nodded and jerked when she hit a sensitive spot on his back. "I haven't seen him in a long time. He's trying to break from Nigel."

"You believe him?" She tried to watch his profile while cleaning the wounds.

"I do."

She lowered her hands to her lap. "He came here to kill you."

"Nay," he said and turned to look at her over his shoulder. "He came here to kill Serena and you."

"Me? I don't understand."

Cade rose and walked toward the other blankets. He shifted through them and returned with more clothes. He pulled on a tunic of dark blue and stared down at her.

"You're a witch. For some reason Nigel views you and Serena as threats. He wants both of you dead."

Francesca rose on shaky legs and turned her back to Cade so he wouldn't see the doubt on her eyes. Had Nigel seen the same dream that played in her mind every night? Did he know what awaited him if she lived?

The damp, bloody material fell from her hand as her mind raced with possibilities. Serena and her child needed to get to safety, but she knew Serena would never leave Drogan.

"I won't let him harm you."

She turned at Cade's words to find he had changed into clean breeches.

"I promise," he said. "Nigel won't get near you."

Francesca smiled at his words, because she knew he meant them. "Thank you."

"As soon as the storm clears, you and Serena need to get to Phineas' and stay on the isle until the threat from Nigel is over."

If only she were able to do as he asked. "If Liam is trying to break from Nigel, will he join us?"

"Nay," Cade said and bent to stroke the fire. "He took a great chance talking to me at all. Nigel doesn't let anyone leave. He'll be after Liam soon."

She returned to her seat across the fire. Drogan had never known if Cade left or if Nigel had let him go. "Did you leave Nigel?"

He refused to look up from the fire, as if he were trying to determine how he would answer.

"You think I'm still in league with him," Cade said after a moment.

It wasn't a question. She knew that no matter how she answered, he wouldn't believe her. "You've never told anyone. Not even Drogan. What would you have people believe?"

"I don't know." He blew out a breath and sat on the rock.

The darkness that was always near him seemed to wrap around him like a comfortable cloak. He had drawn it into himself without even knowing it.

"Why do you talk to me but not Drogan?" she asked.

His eyes closed for the barest moment. "I wish I knew."

A thrill raced through her. Could he be as affected by her as she was by him? He had nearly kissed her, but did that mean anything? She had no experience with men other than what she had observed through the years. And all that did was confuse her even more.

"Have you seen Drogan's son?"

Something flashed in Cade's eyes. "Nay."

"You should. For Drogan."

"It's because of Drogan that I'm staying away."

"Is it? Or is it because you fear what you'll see in his eyes?"

Cade jerked to his feet, and she instantly regretted her words.

"Tell me you don't feel it," Cade demanded, his voice harsh.

She wanted to think he spoke about the desire, but she knew he referred to the darkness. "I feel it."

He squeezed his eyes shut for a moment before he pinned her with his gaze. "If anyone spends too much time with me, they'll begin to feel despair and heartache. The darkness will latch onto them, causing them nothing but pain until they either turn to the evil or take their own life. Is that what you want me to give Drogan?"

"I had no idea."

"I feel your magic."

Her heart skipped a beat at his murmured words. "What does it feel like?"

"Hope. Pleasure. Happiness. Stay near me long enough, and I'll leave you empty."

Before she could respond, he stalked to the opening of the cave. She wanted to go to him, to tell him he was wrong. The rigid way he held his body kept her in place. She had only wanted to get to know him better, but had succeeded in pushing him farther away.

Francesca tucked her hair behind her ear and lay on her side. She used her arm as her pillow. Over and over she replayed her conversation with Cade about Nigel, Liam and Drogan. Still, she wasn't able to come up with an answer that would save everyone's life. Liam was someone she had never seen in her dreams, and he could be nothing more than a messenger sent to give Cade news.

But what if he wasn't?

Cade trusted him, but it was difficult for her to trust anyone associated with Nigel.

Except Cade.

Despite the darkness around Cade, there was an honesty in his gaze that was hard to miss. His love for his friends, and the way he risked his life to protect them, brought tears to her eyes. He was in such pain, the loneliness eating away at him, that he didn't know what to do when he was around another person. It explained his gruff behavior, but not why she was drawn to him.

She'd known the day would be filled with adventure from the frantic dream she'd had the night before. But she had never seen the wolf. Or Liam. Or Cade's near kiss.

What else hadn't been shown to her?

That in itself worried her. She was never shown all, but she had always been shown the important parts. All that had played in her dream last night was the storm. And her racing heart.

The storm had arrived early, and fiercer than anyone had expected. The lightning had yet to let up. But that wasn't what caused her heart to race. Cade was responsible for that.

Francesca didn't want to feel that way towards him. She had distanced herself from everyone over the past several years. It made no sense that she would want to get close to Cade. She had an important role to play, and becoming attached to Cade would only complicate matters. Even as she told herself to stay away from him, her body cried out for his touch, his heat.

Her eyes closed as she remembered the feel of his thumb on her lips. Her breath quickened, and her breasts swelled. How could one touch do that to her? One simple touch.

Oh, how she longed for him to touch her again, to kiss her, caress her. She wanted him to pin her against the tree once more so she could feel his hard length along hers.

Francesca squeezed her eyes closed and went over the magic she had instilled in the castle. She had been over everything thrice, but once more couldn't hurt. The more magic that surrounded Wolfglynn, the better.

Chapter Six

Moments ticked into hours, and still the storm didn't abate. The wind would die down only to return with more force than before. Lightning struck trees and water. The thick, black clouds bathed the land in darkness, and it was only midday.

During it all, Cade refused to leave his spot at the entrance to the cave. He couldn't be near Francesca. She made him look too deep into his heart and wish for things he couldn't have. She dared to look him in the eye with others turned away.

It made him long to be the man he used to be, the man he was before Nigel. That man would have courted her, taken her in his arms and kissed her until she was breathless. That man wouldn't let anything stand in the way of making her his. That man would give her a future.

There was no future for him. He fully expected to die in the battle with Nigel. But not before he killed Nigel himself. Cade longed for death, to ease the torment in his soul. But before he went, he planned on giving Gerard, Drogan, Liam and all the others some peace and a future without Nigel.

It was the least he could do.

Unable to stand it a moment longer, Cade turned to look at Francesca. He had expected her to follow him, her questions continuing. Yet she hadn't. He thanked her for that at the same time he cursed her for giving up so easily.

You want her to give up.

Aye, he did. Didn't he?

"We can turn her," the darkness whispered.

Cade tamped down the voice. Francesca was on her side, her lips parted slightly as she slept. Cade was walking towards her before he knew what he was doing. He squatted beside her and lifted a fiery lock.

He half-expected it to burn him. But the red tresses were as soft as silk and as cool as the rain. The dying firelight brought out the gold highlights in her hair.

"Beautiful," he murmured.

Yet the word seemed lacking when he described her. She was utterly magnificent. He wanted to make slow, sweet love to her while looking in her eyes. He wanted to hear her scream his name when she climaxed.

And he wanted to hold her in his arms, their bodies entwined as they talked until dawn.

Cade had accepted his life. After all, it had been the decisions he'd made that brought him the darkness. But one look at Francesca, and he wanted more. Much more.

"You're something I can never have," he whispered.

He was only torturing himself by staying with her. He should get a message to Drogan that she was safe, but every time he started out of the cave, he would stop.

It was selfish of him, but he wasn't ready to return the witch. He prayed the storm lasted into the night, for it would give him a few more hours with her. A few more hours in which he could etch her beauty into his mind and hold onto it in the cold, lonely nights ahead.

"Take her," the darkness urged. *"She won't stop you."*

Stop.

"You want her. Make her yours."

Enough!

Cade straightened and fisted his hands as he fought against the darkness. He wouldn't sully Francesca with his evil. She was too good, too pure. She deserved so much more than him.

Fight the darkness. Fight for her.

If only he could, but Cade knew the darkness had become too strong. He held onto his humanity by a thin thread that unraveled more each day. He would be lucky if he was still in his right mind by the time Nigel arrived.

Cade gathered more wood from the back of the cave and kept the fire built up. He settled across the fire from Francesca and grabbed one of the small pieces of wood he always kept with him.

He pulled the small dagger from his boot and began to carve. He never knew what he was going to shape, only that he loved to do it. His dagger had whittled anything from cats to boats to a dragon. In his younger days, he had carved larger pieces, loving the feel of the wood in his hand and watching it take shape.

The feel of the blade chipping away at the wood calmed his soul. It was one of the reasons the darkness hadn't taken complete control of him yet. He had learned what carving could do for him and made sure he did it whenever he could.

Which was often.

The piece of wood was no longer than his hand, and he worked it easily. It was a few moments later that he realized this would turn out to be a wolf. He had done several wolves since guarding Drogan's forest, but this wasn't one of the beautiful, wild creatures he had seen on many occasions. The wolf in his hand was the angry, vengeful wolf he had wounded earlier.

He had learned early on not to try and stop once a shape had begun in the wood. His hands had a mind of their own—the need to whittle whatever creature or object was there to give him peace.

Whether he liked what he carved or not, he did not slow. He let the wolf take shape in slow, measured strokes of his blade. By the time he finished, the menacing look of the wolf was obvious in its snarling teeth and crouched position. Cade tossed it aside and glanced at Francesca. She still slept peacefully.

The lightning had slowed, though the thunder was unrelenting. The wind continued to blow the rain sideways, drenching everything. Sometime during the storm, the sun had sunk into the horizon, and night had fallen.

Cade slid down the rock until his back and head rested against it. He closed his eyes, knowing he wouldn't sleep the night through, but trying to find a few hours rest. Part of him wished Francesca were awake. She had a bright mind and a seductive smile, as if she knew some secret he did not. He wanted to know all there was about her, but in return, she would ask him questions he couldn't—and wouldn't—answer.

He released a sigh and let his eyes close.

"Fool," he murmured to himself.

As soon as the storm stopped, he was getting himself as far away from Francesca as he could. No more staring at her, no more yearning to talk to her, to touch her. To kiss her.

He groaned at the thought of her naked in his arms, her head thrown back as he thrust into her body. His cock swelled with need and lust. He gripped his throbbing rod and shifted it to relieve some of the aching. But it only made it worse.

God, how he wanted her. To nuzzle her neck and nip at the delicate skin behind her ear. He wanted to cup her breasts and run his thumb over her nipples, watching them harden before his eyes. Only then would he take one in his mouth, swirling his tongue around the tiny bud.

Cade broke out into a cold sweat, his body demanding release. His heart pounded mercilessly in his chest, and the darkness clawed at him, hungering for a taste of the sweet witch across the fire.

Nay.

"Yes," the darkness hissed. *"She's a tasty morsel."*

Cade inhaled deeply and pushed all thoughts of Francesca and her body from his mind. It was the hardest thing he had done, but he knew that, to ensure her safety, he had no other choice.

His body shook with the desire pumping through his veins as the darkness continued to goad him into taking her. Moments, hours, or days could have passed. When Cade opened his eyes, he was once more in control.

The darkness had claimed another part of his soul, but it was a piece Cade had gladly given up to keep the darkness away from Francesca. With his mind clear, he closed his eyes and prayed he didn't dream of a witch with fiery hair and tawny eyes.

* * * * *

Francesca bit her lip to hold back her scream as she sat up, clutching the blanket to her chest. While sweat covered her body, the dream replayed in her mind.

As she had done every night since she was ten, she had dreamed of Nigel. But this time was different. Instead of seeing how he would die, she had watched the world go deathly black and eerily quiet.

In the darkness was evil that hovered around her, clawing at her skin. She screamed over and over again, but no sound ever came from her. She'd learned to accept and translate the dreams that her magic had given her, but this dream left a cold weight in her belly.

The fire cracked. She turned and saw Cade resting across from her. She watched him for several moments, praying he didn't wake. He would want to know what was wrong, and she couldn't tell him.

She licked lips cracked dry and stumbled to her feet. Using her hand to hold her up on shaky legs, she walked to where Cade kept the food and saw a jug of wine. She grabbed it and held it against her as she staggered back to her spot.

Her knees gave out before she reached the fire, and she crawled the rest of the way, pulling the wine after her. Her hands shook so badly, it took her several tries to uncork the jug. When she finally got it opened, the dark liquid spilled past her lips to run down her chin.

She drank deeply, letting the wine burn her throat as it slid to her stomach. It didn't take long for the alcohol to begin to dull her senses. Only in dire need did she ever touch wine or ale, but the dream had called for nothing else.

She wiped the back of her hand over her mouth and took in a shaky breath. The effects of the dream were loosening. To ensure she was able to let go of the fear, she drank more of the wine until the fire began to blur. Only then did she lower the jug.

A glance down showed the blanket had long ago slipped free. No man had ever seen her body. She looked at Cade sleeping quietly.

And no man ever would.

She hated the disappointment that realization brought. Though she didn't want to go back to sleep, the wine made it impossible to keep her eyes open. She nestled down and slid the blanket over her once more. Just before she closed her eyes, she looked over at Cade again.

Only to find him staring at her.

Chapter Seven

Cade sat up, unsure of what he'd just witnessed. Magic vibrating around him had woken him, but it was the sight of Francesca shaking and barely able to stand, her fear palpable, that held him immobile.

His first thought had been to go to her, to help her, but then he wondered if he would only make matters worse. He fisted his hands and watched as she drank the wine in such a rush that the liquid ran down her chin to drip onto her breasts.

The need to lick the wine from her skin had made his balls tighten. But when the blanket fell, revealing a body he'd only dreamt of, he forgot how to breathe.

Full, luscious breasts swayed in the firelight, her pale nipples hardening in the cool sea breeze. Her long, lean legs were tucked beneath her, but he still glimpsed a patch of red curls betwixt her legs.

His mouth watered, his cock thickened.

His body *hungered*.

Her gaze had slid to him, her brow furrowing as she saw him. He had kept his eyes parted only a slit, but when she had looked at him with such regret, such sorrow, he had nearly gone to her.

His muscles had bunched, ready to rise and take the only thing he had ever found he wanted more than peace.

Francesca.

Thankfully, she'd lain down and pulled the blanket over her mouthwatering body. Only then did Cade open his eyes. His heart had stopped when their gazes collided, but then her lids had closed and her breathing quickly evened into sleep.

Cade sat up and ran a hand down his face. He had always heard a man would have to face his toughest temptation to garner a spot into Heaven. It seemed even the ones destined for Hell were forced to endure such enticement.

He rose to his feet and went to kneel beside Francesca. A soft sheen of sweat glistened over her skin.

"What did you dream about, witch?"

Whatever she'd seen had frightened her. He knew little of Francesca and her powers. Maybe she had such nightmares every night, but something told Cade that wasn't true. On one of his visits to the forest after Serena had nearly died, Drogan had told Cade what Serena was. A witch, Drogan had said. A witch who had magic.

Cade had wanted to ask so many questions but had stayed hidden, listening as Drogan spoke of Serena's power to see people's deaths.

Drogan had never said, but Cade suspected Serena had seen Cade's death. He didn't need a witch to tell him how he was going to die, however. He knew exactly how his time on earth would end. And who would end it.

If Serena had power, it would only follow that Francesca did as well. Could dreams be her power? He wanted to know, but some instinct cautioned him about asking.

Cade rose and backed away from Francesca. Only a few hours had passed, but he didn't try to sleep for a second time. Rest would not come to him again, not this night. Instead, he took up a position at the cave's entrance and watched the storm.

It was just after dawn when the storm finally broke. Cade was both happy and sad, because he knew there was no longer a reason for Francesca to stay with him.

She had woken earlier. He'd heard her moving about, but he didn't chance looking at her. The darkness would rise up in him again, and he didn't know how much longer he could hold it at bay. The witch had been nice to him, trusting him as no one had in a very, very long time. He didn't wish to harm her in any way.

And the darkness would certainly hurt her.

The soft scent of lilacs reached him. He inhaled her fragrance, the scent that was hers alone. As much as he hated to admit it, he was going to miss the tingle on his skin her magic caused, the smell of lilacs, her voice, and the way her soft body felt against his.

"I've never seen a storm so bad," she said as she came to stand beside him.

Cade thought about ignoring her but realized he couldn't. "It's not over yet, but the lightning has stopped so you can return to the castle."

"I see more clouds over the water. We could be in for another storm."

He pressed his lips together. There was something at work here, and it wasn't the witches.

Nigel.

"Yes, yes," the darkness cackled.

"You need to get to the castle soon," Cade said as he stood and faced her. "The danger out here will only worsen."

Her tawny gaze studied him for a moment. "You don't think the storm is natural."

"You said yourself you've never seen one so bad. Lightning and thunder that stayed in one place despite the howling wind?"

She licked her lips, and he tried not to look at her mouth, but he couldn't seem to help himself.

"There are more clouds," she said again. "Another storm."

He forced his gaze to her eyes. "Perhaps."

"Is it Nigel?"

"I believe so."

Her brow puckered. "Why? Why does he want to keep us here? None of us have tried to leave."

It was then Cade realized why Nigel had brought the storm. "It will keep you at Wolfglynn and me out of the forest, or so he thinks."

She glanced away at him, but not before he saw something shift in her gaze.

"Do you know something, witch?"

"Maybe Nigel wants to ensure that no one gets to the castle."

Cade folded his arms over his chest. The only ones he knew who would come to Wolfglynn were Gerard and Grayson. Since Gerard had his family, it must be Grayson Nigel was after. Though Cade didn't know everything that had happened with Grayson, Drogan had told him enough during his many trips to the forest to try and lure Cade to the castle.

"Can Grayson help?" he asked.

Francesca shook her head. "I fear he and his men will only end up dead."

"Then perhaps it's better if the storm keeps them away."

"You don't know Grayson. He's loyal to Drogan. Completely."

Cade drummed his fingers on his arm. "Even though Grayson is a lord himself, and a knight for Drogan no more?"

"Even though he is a lord. Drogan sheltered Grayson, believed in him. But more importantly, Drogan knew Grayson held secrets and didn't pry."

"Grayson's wife, she's a witch as well?"

Francesca nodded. "Adrianna. Serena met her when she and Drogan were coming to Wolfglynn."

Liam had said Nigel wanted the witches dead. If Grayson managed to get in, then all three would be within striking distance.

"How powerful is Adrianna?"

Francesca lifted a shoulder in a shrug. "I don't know. All of us have some sort of magic. Why?"

"Liam said Nigel wanted the witches dead. What if the storm isn't to keep Grayson from helping Drogan, but keeping Adrianna from reaching you and Serena?"

Francesca's eyes widened. "By the saints."

Cade knew he only had once choice. "Are you sure Grayson is coming?"

"Drogan got a missive from him a month ago telling him he was on his way."

Shite! "Go to the castle, witch. Whatever you do, keep Drogan and Serena inside those walls."

"I've used my magic. The castle should be safe from Nigel."

"Nothing will stop Nigel from getting inside the castle if he wants in." He gave her one last look and started out of the castle. Her hand closed over his arm, halting him instantly. He looked over his shoulder at her.

"What are you going to do?"

"I'm going to try and get to Grayson and Adrianna before Nigel."

Her brow furrowed. "You're one man, Cade. You can't fight an army."

With the darkness with him, he *was* an army. "Remember what I said, witch."

He raced from the cave before he gave in to the desire to kiss the beautiful, alluring, altogether too tempting witch.

Cade leapt over rocks and ignored the pull of his wounds. The injury on his leg throbbed, and he felt a trickle of blood, letting him know he had reopened it, but there was no time to stop. Already it might be too late.

He was risking everything leaving Wolfglynn to find Grayson and Adrianna, but Nigel needed the witches dead because he feared them. So it was up to Cade to make sure they stayed alive.

Cade jumped over puddles and fallen trees. He skirted the castle through the forest. A glance at the castle told him with the lessening rain, men would be moving about. He just hoped Francesca got to Drogan and Serena in time.

* * * * *

Francesca stood in the cave and watched Cade race away from her. The resolve and fury in his gaze had given her pause, but she realized it was because he feared he might already be too late to help Grayson and Adrianna.

"Be careful, Cade," she said as he disappeared into the forest.

Francesca made sure the fire was out before she headed to the castle. The rain had slowed, but by the time she reached the kitchen entrance, she was drenched again.

As she passed servants, she asked them to find Drogan and Serena. Then she headed to the chamber she used on the occasions she stayed at Wolfglynn. Those occasions were rare, but sometimes the weather, like last night's, prevented her from making the trip back to the isle.

Phineas, Drogan's uncle, was lord of the isle, and though he told her she didn't have to return, she did. Phineas was like a father to her. He had known what she was and loved her for it. He didn't exploit her gifts, but helped to hide her from a world that didn't understand what she was. For that, she owed him her life. So she returned to him every day to dine with him and talk about the day.

She sighed as she reached the landing to her chamber. Had Phineas fared well in the storm? He seemed to grow weaker every day, though he refused to admit it. He was always ready with a smile, greeting each day as if it were his last.

Francesca closed the door to her chamber behind her and quickly removed her sodden gown. She longed to take a leisurely bath, but there was no time.

She threw open the trunk before the bed and found a gown of dark green that she hurried to put on after a clean chemise and stockings. She pulled on her shoes and was combing the tangles from her hair when there was a knock on her door.

"Enter," she called.

Drogan and Serena stood in the doorway.

"Where were you?" Serena asked as she rushed to Francesca.

Francesca smiled. "I've been fine. Cade took me to a cave."

"Cade?" Drogan asked. "Cade? The same Cade in the forest?"

Francesca nodded. "I'll tell you everything, but first, Cade made me promise that you both would stay inside the castle until he returned."

Serena shrugged and glanced at her husband. "All right."

"Why?" Drogan asked. "And how will we know when Cade returns."

Francesca sank onto her bed and sighed. She knew she couldn't tell Drogan anything until he promised to stay in the castle. It would be just like him to go after Cade to help. "Promise me you'll stay."

Serena nudged her husband.

Drogan blew out a breath. "Alright. I vow to stay in the castle until Cade returns."

She smiled then because she had fulfilled her promise to Cade. So much had happened yesterday and last night. So much she hadn't had time to think about.

"Fran."

She blinked and looked at Drogan. "I apologize. It's been…eventful."

"How 'eventful'?" he asked with a narrowed gaze.

It was all she could do not to laugh. "Cade didn't touch me." That wasn't precisely true, but Drogan didn't need to know everything.

"I see."

Was that disappointment she saw in his eyes?

"What did happen?" Serena asked. She had her black hair in a braid that fell over her shoulder.

Francesca sighed. "You know of the wolf attack."

"Aye," Drogan said. "None of the wolves have ever attacked."

"Cade said it wasn't one of your wolves."

Drogan began to pace. "It was larger. And solid black. There are no black wolves around here. That doesn't mean one couldn't have roamed into our forest."

"Cade said it came from Nigel."

Drogan stopped in his tracks and stared at her.

Francesca folded her hands in her lap. "I saw Cade fight the wolf, and I followed him when he walked away. I wanted to talk to him some more."

"I don't understand," Serena said. "You said 'some more' as if you've spoken with Cade before."

"She has, love," Drogan said. "Yesterday morning she came upon Cade, and he spoke with her."

Serena shook her head. "I can hardly believe it. He's never spoken with anyone at Wolfglynn."

"I surprised him," Francesca said. "At any rate, I followed him, and just as I was about to ask him about the wolf, he heard something."

Drogan grasped one of the chairs before the hearth and lowered himself into it. "There's something else out there?"

"Before Cade was able to see what it was, the storm broke. He took me to a cave that he uses."

Serena placed her hands on her husband's shoulders. "That's where you've been all night? We've been worried sick."

"Aye, I've been there. Cade left again, though. He wanted to find out what else was in the trees."

"What was it?" Drogan asked.

"A man. Liam."

Drogan shook his head and shrugged. "The name means nothing."

"It meant something to Cade. He knew him and trusted him. Apparently this Liam was sent by Nigel."

"To kill me?" Drogan asked with a sneer.

Francesca licked her lips. "Nay. To kill me and Serena. He wants us dead."

Drogan paled. "Why?"

"I don't know. Liam told Cade he was breaking from Nigel, and he was giving Cade the warning that Nigel was on his way here to kill us."

"I take it Cade believed him?" Serena asked.

Francesca nodded. "I asked him the same question, and he does."

"So where is Cade now?" Drogan asked. "In the forest? I need to speak to him."

She exchanged a glance with Serena. This was the part she had been dreading. Drogan was not going to react well to the news that he'd been tricked to staying in the castle.

"Drogan, stop scowling," Serena scolded. "Let Fran finish."

Francesca gave her a smile of thanks. "Cade had a suspicion this morning that the storm wasn't natural."

"Aye, I had my own suspicions," Drogan said. "It wasn't ordinary."

"And neither is the storm that's heading this way," Serena said.

Francesca nodded. "We deduced that as well. I thought it was Nigel's ploy to keep us all here, but Cade realized the true reason for the storms."

"He's keeping Grayson away," Drogan said and surged to his feet. He raked a hand through his hair. "Cade went after Grayson, didn't he?"

Francesca nodded. "He realized Adrianna would be in as much danger as we are. He's trying to reach them before Nigel."

Drogan turned and punched the small table that stood between the chairs. It splintered and crashed to the floor.

"I should be with him." Drogan's voice was harsh, haunted.

Serena rubbed his back as if she could take away his pain.

Francesca rose to her feet. "It's because he cares for you so much that he is going to such lengths to keep you safe. Respect what he's doing."

Drogan lifted his golden gaze to hers, his eyes sparkling with anger. "He's going to get himself killed. He doesn't stand a chance alone."

She knew that all too well, but something in Cade's gaze had told her he knew he would be all right. She had to trust in him, trust that he could get Grayson and Adrianna to Wolfglynn safely.

"He's going to die." Dorgan's voice was harsh with emotion.

"No, he won't," Serena said.

Francesca jerked her gaze to her friend. "You've seen it? You've seen how he will die?"

Chapter Eight

As he ran, Cade loosened his hold on the darkness. He needed to find Grayson, and the only way to do that was with the darkness. He just prayed he'd be able to pull the evil back in.

"Yes," the darkness cooed. "Grayson is surrounded. He's going to die!"

Where?

"Not far. To your left."

Cade grimaced as the darkness fought to control him, to turn him into the very thing that Nigel wanted, needed. But Cade fought it.

He tripped over a fallen log and landed hard on his side. Mud and leaves clung to his tunic as he jumped to his feet. He followed the darkness's orders and turned left even as he continued to fight the evil.

Cade lost track of time. He was so absorbed in fighting the darkness he had no idea where he was, but he had to let the darkness guide him, to find Grayson and Adrianna.

"Yes! Fight. Kill them. Kill them!" the darkness screamed.

Cade came to a halt and moved behind a tree. He closed his eyes and struggled to get his breathing under control. His leg ached mercilessly, and his side and lungs burned from his exertion.

"*Join Nigel's army*," the darkness urged. *"Be the man you were destined to be."*

Cade ignored the voice in his head and took stock of Nigel's men. He had indeed sent an army. The men slowly made their way around Grayson's camp, swords drawn and ready. Cade needed to get to Grayson. He didn't want to fight Nigel's men until Grayson and Adrianna had started toward Wolfglynn.

Shite.

There was only one thing for Cade to do, and it was almost too risky to consider. But he owed it to Drogan. To Francesca.

He closed his eyes and let the darkness surround him like a shadowy mist. It became difficult to breathe, to think. He pictured Grayson, but his face quickly disappeared. He thought of Drogan, but even his closest friend faded.

Then his thoughts turned to Francesca, her soft lips and scent that drove him mad with lust. Only then was he able to remember who he was, and what he needed to do.

Cade took a deep breath and stepped away from the tree. He walked among Nigel's army, never once seen. He stepped through the perimeter Grayson had set up around his camp. Grayson's men had their swords drawn, because even though they couldn't see anything, they felt the evil of Nigel's army.

He continued on until he came to the large tent. Only when he was inside did he force the darkness away. For a moment, the darkness rebelled, and Cade thought he might lose all. With his hands fisted and his jaw clenched, he turned his mind once more to Francesca, praying the thought of her would somehow help get the darkness under control.

Little by little, the darkness was tamped down. When Cade opened his eyes, it was to find Grayson standing in front of him with a sword at his throat.

"Who are you?" Grayson demanded.

Cade looked at the black-haired warrior with his silver eyes. Grayson would have fit into their group easily, which was why Drogan had taken such a liking to the man.

"You know me," Cade answered.

Grayson narrowed his gaze and swore. "Cade?"

He was impressed. The warrior had only seen him once, and it had been a year ago. "Aye."

"How did you get past my guards?"

Cade glanced over Grayson's shoulder to find a woman with golden hair staring at him with probing blue eyes. Adrianna, he presumed. "It isn't just your guards I got past, but an army as well."

"Damn." Grayson lowered his sword and raked a hand through his hair. "You were right, Drina."

The woman smiled and placed her hand on Grayson's arm. "Of course I was right." Her gaze moved to Cade. "I sense a great...darkness around you."

Cade took a step back and turned to Grayson. "It's better for all if you keep your distance. There isn't much time. You need to get the witch to Wolfglynn posthaste."

"Why? What's out there?"

"Nigel."

Grayson swore again and sheathed his sword. "The bastard had the chance to kill me before."

"He doesn't want to kill you," Cade said. "He wants the witches dead. All of them."

Adrianna's face paled. "We have no power over him."

Cade shrugged. "He thinks differently. Already he's sent someone to kill Serena and Francesca. I stopped them."

"The storm was courtesy of Nigel, then," Adrianna said.

Cade gave a quick nod. "There's another on the way."

"I know," Adrianna said. "I smell it."

Before Cade could ask what she meant, Grayson spoke. "Then we battle the army."

"Nay." Cade made his fingers unclench. "You'll be killed."

"Someone has to battle them."

"Someone will." Cade had no intention of telling Grayson his plans. "I'll create a diversion in the middle of Nigel's army. It'll divert attention to me. Meanwhile, you need to get Adrianna to Wolfglynn. Don't stop. Not for the weather or anything that might get in your way."

Grayson nodded. "I will tell my men to help you."

"Nay. I don't want your men mistaking me for one of Nigel's. Have them stand down, but continue to guard the camp. When it's clear, they can make their way to Drogan's."

Adrianna walked around her husband until she stood in front of Cade. Her blue eyes held his as if she were searching his soul. "You plan on taking the whole of Nigel's army yourself?"

"You can't," Grayson said. "You'll never survive."

Cade shrugged. "You leave that to me. Now, there's no more time for talking."

He lifted the flap and strode from the tent before they could ask more questions. He prayed Grayson did as he asked, because if Grayson didn't, Nigel would kill Adrianna. Though Cade hadn't figured out why Nigel wanted the witches dead, he would ensure they lived at all costs. Anything to anger Nigel.

As Cade walked through Grayson's camp, men turned to stare at him. He saw the fear, the unease that rippled in their eyes when they looked at him. They needed to fear him. Unleashing the darkness, even the little that he had, had made it near impossible to take control again. Year after year, he had never let it loose. He had fought it, screamed at it. But never had he let it go.

And now he was about to unleash it.

Cade had wanted to save it until the battle with Nigel, but he couldn't. The witches needed to be kept safe. Francesca needed to be kept safe.

A wave of longing surged through him just thinking of her. He should have kissed her when he'd had the chance. He should have tasted her sweet lips, caressed her curves. Because once he unleashed the darkness, there would be no turning back. He would become what he feared most.

He had been preparing to die from the moment the darkness entered his soul. He just hadn't counted on meeting someone like Francesca.

Walking to the edge of Grayson's camp, he still felt the eyes of the men on him. Uneasy, fearful. They had a right to fear him. If they knew what he was about to let free, they would run for their lives.

Cade stopped at the perimeter of the camp, near two knights. His gaze was on the gently rolling hills and the boundary of the forest, where Nigel's army waited.

"Whatever you hear, whatever you see, don't leave this camp," he told them without looking at the men. "Stay here, and don't let anything through."

He reached back and unsheathed his knives as he took a deep breath. It was strange that after all these years of fighting the evil, he was about to give it free reign. He didn't like the fear that fluttered in his stomach at the prospect of becoming what he hated the most.

Francesca.

He didn't know her, didn't understand what she was, but somehow she'd managed to touch him as no other person ever had. The witches needed to be kept alive. At all costs. He only wished he knew why Nigel wanted them dead so badly.

Cade twirled his knives as he stepped away from Grayson's camp. Nigel's men began moving about. Cade smiled, eager to feel his blade sink into flesh.

"Yes, yes! Blood. Drench your blades in blood," the darkness urged.

"Come out, come out wherever you are," Cade taunted Nigel's men.

It took little effort to call forth the darkness. One moment he was walking towards the army, and the next his swords were flying, a red haze descending over his eyes.

* * * * *

"By all that's holy," Grayson murmured as he watched Cade walk into the middle of Nigel's men.

Adrianna tugged on his arm. "Grayson, we need to go."

He couldn't take his eyes from Cade. His blades moved so quickly and proved so deadly that they were a blur. Nigel's men surrounded Cade, pinning him in a tight circle, but he continued to slice and thrust his knives, spinning about as if he weren't quite human.

"You said you sensed darkness," he murmured to his wife.

"Aye," she said. "There is something evil, dark, inside him."

"He had control over it when he got into camp."

Drina blew out a soft breath. "It's like he's on the edge of a blade, Grayson. One slip, and the darkness will claim him."

Grayson glanced at his wife. Her voice held a note of sadness he hadn't expected. He turned back to Cade and watched him. "He let go of the control, didn't he?"

"Aye." Adrianna's reply was barely above a whisper.

Grayson didn't like the idea of leaving such a great warrior alone, but Cade had sacrificed his very soul to protect Adrianna. He turned his back on the battle and adjusted the reins in his hand.

"Ready?" he asked.

Adrianna nodded. "Absolutely."

"I'll get you to Wolfglynn, my love."

"I don't doubt it," she said and flashed him a grin. "Now come, we have another storm to ride through."

Chapter Nine

Francesca stared out of the tower window, hoping for a sign of Cade. After Serena had confessed that Cade wouldn't die in this battle, they had tried to get her to eat, but Francesca couldn't stomach the thought of food.

It wasn't just the idea of Cade fighting against Nigel's men—it was the dream. The dream where fear and evil had clawed at her, tearing her skin.

"I thought I might find you up here."

She glanced over her shoulder to see Serena walk towards her. "Did you see how Cade will die?"

Serena came to stand beside her, their hands side by side on the cool stones of the castle as they gazed out the window. "Why do you want to know?"

How could Francesca explain it? Cade's predicament was something she shouldn't dabble in, yet she found she couldn't help herself. She was drawn to him like a moth to flame.

"Fran?"

She sighed and shrugged. "I don't know. I can't explain it, really. If you could look into his eyes and see his pain, his loneliness, then you might understand."

"I think I know what you mean. It's the darkness, isn't it? Do you feel it when you're around him?"

She nodded. "Did you feel Drogan's?"

"A little, but then again, the darkness wasn't as strong with Drogan as it is with Cade. I'm glad you got him to speak with you. Cade needs a friend."

Francesca faced Serena. "He's risking everything to save us."

"I know. It's driving Drogan daft. He won't stop pacing the battlements."

"You aren't going to tell me how Cade is going to die, are you?"

Serena smiled sadly. "I lied in your chamber. I haven't touched Cade, so I cannot look into his future to see his death."

How could Francesca have forgotten such a tiny detail? She dug her fingers into the stone and tried to calm her racing heart. "Cade could die."

"He most likely will, and I'm sorry for that. What I did, I did for selfish reasons, Fran. If Drogan suspected Cade wouldn't come out of this battle, promise or not, he would go out there to help him."

"I understand. You have a family. You're looking out for the interests of your future."

"But you don't agree with me."

"It isn't for me to agree or disagree." She turned back to the window, the need to see Cade growing with each beat of her heart.

"I'm sorry."

So was Francesca. After a few moments, Serena left the tower. Normally Francesca loved her company, but there was too much on her mind and in her heart that she couldn't share. She needed time to think, to consider the awful dream that had come to her the night before.

And how it was tied to Cade.

She couldn't quite identify the connection, but she knew that somehow it involved Cade. Always before, she had seen the battle with Nigel, seen how she would triumph over the evil. Always it ended at the same moment as her life would.

Her death was something she had known of since she was ten summers. She had never feared it or regretted anything. Though her dreams had never shown her how she would come to battle Nigel, or even how he came into such evil, she knew she could end it all.

And she would.

Nigel was a scourge on the earth, and he needed to be wiped away. Because of what the future held for her, she had never let herself get close to anyone other than Phineas. The old man had been her rock, holding her in the middle of the night when her dreams had shown her horrors she couldn't speak about.

Phineas never asked about her dreams, just held her, soothing her until she was able to sleep once more. As she had gotten older, she had learned to cope with the dreams herself, but always he knew when they came to her.

Francesca leaned her forehead against the stones. Why had the dream changed? The only explanation she could come up with was that something else had changed, too. And that something had to be Cade.

Cade made an effort to keep away from anyone and everyone. Yet, somehow, she had managed to find him and speak to him. Could that small gesture have been enough to change the course of the future?

She would know when she dreamed again. It had been a long time since she had been afraid to sleep, but the thought of repeating the dream left her in a cold sweat.

A shudder racked her body as she recalled the feel of the evil ripping the flesh from her body, her silent screams into the inky gloom. Despair, terror and hopelessness had consumed her. She had never felt such stark emotions before. And she never wanted to again.

Lightening zigzagged across the sky a heartbeat before thunder boomed. Almost instantly, the rain began.

Just like yesterday.

Nigel must have a hand in it. To be able to call the weather meant he was much more powerful than any of them had realized.

"Cade, where are you?" she whispered.

The wind drove the rain into the window, but still she didn't move. She squinted through the rain in hopes of catching Cade moving through the woods. She knew it was futile, but she couldn't give up.

"Riders," a knight shouted from the gatehouse.

Francesca turned her head to the road that lead to the gates of Wolfglynn. She could just make out two horses, their riders hanging low over the animals' necks as they raced toward the gates.

"Raise the gates," Drogan's voice boomed over the rain.

Francesca saw a long blonde braid as the horses galloped into the bailey. She turned and, with her skirts in her hands, flew down the stairs.

By the time she rushed into the great hall, the couple was being whisked away to find dry clothes. Francesca would have to wait for news of Cade. She resisted the urge to call to them, to ask about Cade. They had ridden in a terrible storm, and they needed to get dry. She could wait. She would have to.

Of a sudden, the blonde stopped on the stairs and turned to her. Their eyes met, and she knew this woman must be Adrianna. Another *bana-bhuidseach*. Francesca should be overjoyed at having another witch so near, but she couldn't get past her worry for Cade.

"Adrianna," Grayson said.

Francesca took a step toward them.

"When we left, he was still alive," Adrianna said to her.

Francesca nodded her thanks. It didn't mean Cade was alive now, but he had been. He still could be.

She met the silver gaze of Grayson and saw the questions in his eyes. She would answer what she could, but she had questions of her own.

Francesca turned to the hearth and took one of the chairs in front of the blazing fire. It seemed wrong that she was warm and dry while Cade was in the thick of battle with a storm raging around him.

"Are you sure nothing happened between you and Cade?"

She jumped at the sound of Drogan's voice. She turned her head to find him standing next to her, watching her intently. "When was the last time you saw him?"

"The day we battled Nigel and Serena almost died. He helped me pick the herbs you sent me to find. My hands were too bloody and swollen to pluck the delicate flowers."

"Did you look into his eyes?"

Drogan's brow furrowed. "I...I don't remember. Why?"

"I have. There is such loneliness in his eyes. He keeps to himself to prevent anyone from coming in contact with the darkness, but in doing so, he is losing himself."

"What do you mean?"

"He needs a friend."

Drogan's face darkened. "I am his friend."

"I know. He knows. I'm talking about someone who doesn't care about the evil that surrounds him. You do care because you've fought your own."

Drogan paced in front of her. "I don't fear being near him, Fran. I've begged him to come in the castle, or to talk to me."

"I know you would welcome him, but in the back of your mind, you would wonder if the darkness would claim you once again. And you would have every right to wonder. The darkness that is with him is much stronger than what you carried. It has nearly taken Cade."

Drogan sank into a chair and sighed. "Is there anything we can do?"

"There is something I can do. I can be there for him."

"If he allows you, you mean," Drogan said.

"I don't mean to give him a choice."

Chapter Ten

Cade stood ready, waiting for the next attack. Only there wasn't one. He looked around at the bodies lying in the soil, the rain washing the blood to mingle with the dirt on the ground.

"We're just getting started," the darkness said.

Cade's body ached, but the need, the thirst for more blood sent him searching the bodies for anyone left alive. As soon as he found one, he sunk his sword into the flesh.

The darkness laughed. *"More, more. More!"*

Cade wanted to ignore the prodding. He wanted to retreat to his cave, to try and push the darkness away. But he feared it was too late.

"It is too late."

He lifted his face to the rain and bellowed as the darkness consumed him. He was powerless to fight it, helpless to do anything other than listen to the bloodlust pumping in his veins.

His gaze turned toward Wolfglynn.

"Yes," the darkness hissed. *"Kill them. Kill them all!"*

Chapter Eleven

Francesca jumped as the lightning struck again and again. The storm hadn't lessened as she'd hoped, but instead grew stronger. The men on the battlements couldn't fight the wind and had retreated to the gatehouse.

After her declaration, Drogan had simply stared at her, as if trying to determine whether she was worthy of Cade. She hoped she was.

A shiver raced down her spine of a sudden.

"Fran?" Drogan asked.

She shrugged. "Only in my dreams do I see the future."

"Have you seen Cade's?"

She looked into Drogan's golden eyes and shook her head. "I wish I could call up the future as easily as Serena does, but I cannot."

Drogan sighed. "Serena sees only death. I don't think you would enjoy that gift."

"I'm not sure anyone truly enjoys their gift, unless they are a healer."

As soon as the words were out of her mouth, the hall began to vibrate with magic—new magic. Francesca rose and turned to the stairs to see Adrianna descending the steps followed by Grayson and Serena.

"I'm a healer," Adrianna said.

Grayson took his wife's hand as they walked towards Francesca and Drogan. "That isn't all she can do."

Adrianna smiled at Grayson. "I can see the future, though only in bits. I sense trouble more than anything else. Trouble that I can help me and mine avoid."

"Did you avoid Nigel's army?" Francesca asked.

Grayson sighed and walked Adrianna to a chair. Once she was seated, he rested his arm on the back. "Nay. Drina predicted the storm, which was why we had stopped to make camp. There was no way we could reach the castle before the storm hit."

"And Cade?" Drogan asked. "He got through the army?"

"Aye," Adrianna said. "He was...." She glanced at Grayson.

"Not himself," Grayson finished for her.

Francesca sank into her chair and gazed into the fire. Cade couldn't have succumbed so soon. He had been strong enough to fight the darkness, to keep it under control.

"Cade let the darkness take him," Francesca said. "It was the only way he could get Adrianna and Grayson to the castle safely."

Drogan swore and entwined his fingers with Serena's. "Are you sure, Fran? You've seen it?"

"Nay, but I don't need to. I warned him that he couldn't battle Nigel's army himself, but he told me he could. The only way that he stood a chance at winning—"

"Was letting the darkness out," Serena said. "Drogan, I'm so sorry."

"What will happen to him now?" Adrianna asked. "Will he return to the castle?"

Drogan raked his free hand down his face. "Cade has never stepped foot inside the castle. I doubt he ever will."

"But he is out there," Grayson said.

Drogan nodded. "He's out there."

Francesca lifted her gaze to Drogan. "You can't hunt him."

"If I don't, he'll kill anyone he comes across."

"Wait," Adrianna said. "I don't understand. The evil I sensed in Cade, are you telling me it has taken over?"

Francesca refused to answer. Until she saw Cade herself, until she saw that the darkness had truly beat him, she would defend him.

"Aye," Drogan said. "Cade...he's been fighting the darkness for many years. To finally give in to it, or to let it win, would mean that his soul is well and truly lost. He's nothing but evil now."

"You don't know that for sure," Francesca argued as she gained her feet. "You can't say that, can't order men to hunt him when you haven't seen him."

Drogan's eyes held pity. "I don't need to see him, Fran. I lived with the darkness myself."

"And you beat it. So can Cade."

"I beat it with Serena. Cade is alone, just as you said. You just told me he was losing himself. That makes it easier for the darkness to take over. There is no hope for Cade."

Francesca hated the helplessness she felt, the utter lack of control over the situation. Silence gripped the hall as the five of them stared at each other. She wanted to argue with Drogan to prove that he was wrong. But she couldn't, not until she found Cade.

"The storm," Adrianna said. "It's getting worse. Something has happened."

Francesca looked at Adrianna to find the blonde witch staring into the distance with a faraway look in her eyes.

Grayson went down on his haunches in front of her. "Drina, what do you see?"

"Anger. The storm is meant to kill."

"Cade," Drogan said softly. "Cade must have destroyed Nigel's army."

Grayson nodded. "It would explain the storm and his anger."

Hope blossomed in Francesca's chest. If Cade had beaten Nigel's army, that meant he was still alive. There was still a chance for him.

A chance for us.

She wasn't sure where that thought had come from, but she couldn't deny it. Though it went against everything she had believed in for so many years, she wanted Cade with a desperation that frightened her.

Adrianna blinked and took a deep breath. When she opened her blue eyes, they were trained on Francesca.

"After all Cade did for us, we need to keep the women safe," Grayson said.

Drogan nodded. "I don't understand why Nigel wants them dead."

"Look what happened when he tried to battle me," Serena said. "I gave you the amulet that saved your life. I had no way of knowing it at the time, but Nigel doesn't know that."

"True," Drogan agreed. "So he fears you three."

Adrianna folded her hands in her lap. "It has been many centuries since any *bana-bhuidseach* have lived together. At one time, the power of all witches could have combined to kill such evil, but I don't know that the three of us could do it."

"I've never used my powers in such a way," Serena admitted.

Francesca shook her head. "Neither have I. I wouldn't know the first thing to do."

"Just as I expected," Adrianna said. "I, also, have never used my power that way. I don't think it's possible. With each death of one of us, our powers have diminished."

"That might be true, my love," Grayson said. "Yet there is no doubt Nigel fears you. We may never know the reason, but I would feel much better knowing you are alive."

Francesca watched the exchange between Grayson and Adrianna with the same envy that she watched Serena and Drogan. There wasn't a future for her, least of all one that included a man who looked at her with such love in his eyes.

"Tell them," Francesca said to Drogan.

Grayson looked from her to Drogan. "Tell us what?"

"Francesca had a dream vision."

She licked her lips. "The only way for Serena and her son to survive Nigel's attack is to hide somewhere. Somewhere Nigel would never be able to find them. I told Drogan he needed to be with them also, but he won't listen to me."

"I need to fight Nigel," Drogan argued.

Francesca faced the man who had grown up more her brother than anything. "You'll end up dead if you aren't with your wife and child."

"Drogan," Serena said. "Listen to Fran. Her powers won't lead her wrong."

"I won't hide while my men fight Nigel."

Francesca knew it was an argument that could go on for days. She looked to Grayson and Adrianna. "The chamber is hidden and protected by my and Serena's magic. It is a good place for Adrianna to hide as well."

"And what of you?" Adrianna asked.

"Of course I'll be in the chamber," she lied smoothly.

Adrianna nodded. "Good. I'll add my magic to the room as well."

"You might want to add it to the castle," Serena said. "Fran and I have put magic all over the castle just in case."

"I will see to it," Drina said.

Francesca could stand it no longer. She had to know what Cade said to Grayson and Adrianna. "You spoke with Cade, aye?"

"Aye," Grayson said.

"What did he say?"

"Only that he would create a diversion that would allow Drina and I to ride for Wolfglynn without being followed."

Francesca gripped her skirts with her fingers. The need to rush to the forest to find Cade was overwhelming. The only thing that stopped her was the men beside her. She knew that

Drogan wouldn't allow her outside, not when he feared Cade had turned.

"I've never seen someone fight like he did," Adrianna said. "Now I understand how his blades could move so quickly. He didn't have to unleash the darkness, but he did it for us. For that, I'll always be thankful."

Grayson nodded. "He did a very brave thing."

"We needed him to fight Nigel," Francesca said, unable to keep the weariness from her voice.

Drogan moved to stand beside her. "We'll figure out a way."

Aye, she would. Francesca forced a grin. "I want each of you to promise me that you'll find your way to the secret chamber as soon as Nigel arrives."

"Aye," Serena and Adrianna said in unison.

Grayson and Drogan exchanged glances but said nothing.

"Grayson? Drogan?" Serena urged. "I'm not going into the chamber without you, Drogan."

"Serena, understand that I cannot, and will not, allow my people to battle Nigel alone," Drogan said.

Francesca knew that Serena and Adrianna would talk their husbands into the chamber. They were *bana-bhuidseach,* after all. "Nigel will be here soon."

"Have you seen it?" Adrianna asked.

She shook her head. "It's only a feeling, but it has strengthened with each passing day."

"I agree with Fran," Serena said. "It's nothing I can put my finger on, but it's like a threat that has been growing in my mind."

"I've felt it as well," Grayson said.

Francesca looked at him. "How is it that I never knew you were *bana-bhuidseach*?"

"I didn't even know," Grayson admitted.

"He can heal himself," Adrianna said. "It comes in handy in battle."

Serena crossed her arms over her chest. "Odd, don't you think, that Nigel would want me, Fran and Drina dead, but not Grayson."

"Not so odd," Drina said. "Nigel had the chance to kill him. They battled, but Nigel didn't realize Grayson's father wasn't dead as he had believed."

"It was my parent's magic, combined with mine and Drina's, that helped me win," Grayson said.

Drina nodded. "That and the fact that after I had put magic into his sword, I also had it blessed by the priest after Grayson told me what happened when Serena gave Drogan the amulet."

"Since we're all in this together, everything needs to be brought out. Fran has had a chance to talk to Cade," Drogan said.

After Francesca told them about Liam and how much stronger Nigel had become, she slipped away from the group. She wandered the corridors of the castle, ignoring the storm and the fear while she worried about Cade.

She found herself standing in a tower that faced the sea. The rain was coming down so hard she couldn't see the isle. Only with the lightning strikes was she able to make out the hulky form of Phineas' castle.

"He's fine," Drogan's voice said from behind her.

She nodded, knowing he was referring to his uncle. "Phineas is a strong man. It's just that I rarely spend so many nights away from him."

Drogan came to stand beside her. "For a man who didn't have any children of his own, he was a father to both of us."

"He's the only father I ever knew."

"How come I never realized you were a witch?"

Francesca shrugged. "I didn't want anyone to know. People react strangely when they discover what I am. I didn't wish to be burned at the stake."

"I wouldn't have, and you know Phineas wouldn't have let me."

She smiled despite herself. "Phineas is very protective. I think it's because of how he found me."

"He told me he found you half drowned. What happened?"

"I don't know. I was so young. I remember my mother's arms around me, but the waves were so high. I was ripped from her. I sometimes still hear her screaming my name in my dreams."

"But your mother was found," Drogan said.

"Aye. She was the reason Phineas came looking for me."

Drogan nodded and crossed his arms over his chest. "I remember your mother. You have her hair. What I recall most was that she never smiled. She would sit in the tower and stare out."

"She was looking for my father."

"He was alive?"

Francesca shrugged. "I don't believe so. I was too young to know why she never spoke of him, but I did hear her and Phineas speaking one day. She told Phineas about a battle my father was in and how he was wounded. She tried to get to him, to save him."

"You don't think she ever did?"

"Nay. I think he died, and I don't think she ever forgave herself for failing him."

For long moments they stood in silence before Drogan spoke again. "I'm glad Cade spoke with you."

She finally turned to look at Drogan. "You've given up on him."

"Nay." He shook his head to punctuate his words. Drogan dropped his arms and sighed. "However, I am being realistic, Fran. You don't know what it's like living with the darkness, and Cade's was always worse than mine. The only way he could have defeated Nigel's army was to unleash it. As strong a man as Cade is, I don't think even he could come back from that."

"You're not even going to try and find out, are you?"

"If he is able to triumph over the darkness, no one will be able to find him."

"And if he hasn't?"

"He'll kill everyone he sees, and he will be looking."

Francesca swallowed. "What happened to him, Drogan? Why is the darkness so strong in him?"

Drogan's eyes shut away all emotion. "That's Cade's story, Fran. He should be the one to tell you."

"Then tell me about Cade. Tell me how he came to be in your small group."

Drogan scratched his chin. "We were the king's assassins. Gerard and I were recruited because of our skill with weapons. For the longest, it was just the two of us. Then one day, Nigel brought Cade.

"We were only a handful of years older than he was, but we had seen so much death that we had aged beyond our years. Cade's eyes were filled with such hope and faith for his future that it nearly killed me the first time he came on assignment with us."

"What happened?" Francesca urged when he paused.

"Cade never questioned our orders. He was there to defend king and country, and he assumed that the orders we got were from the king himself and the person was guilty."

"That wasn't always the case."

Drogan shook his head. "Gerard and I learned that early on. Not every assignment came from the king. We suspected that Nigel forged the missives, but we could never prove it."

"So Cade did his job."

"Aye. As good as Gerard and I are with weapons, Cade has a gift. He did things I had never seen before. His weapons were an extension of him, as if held some kind of power over them to make them do the things he did."

Francesca leaned against the wall, the sensation of the cool, damp stones penetrating her gown. "I've seen him fight. He's breathtaking."

"Which is what caught Nigel's attention. Soon Nigel was sending Cade on special assignments alone. Every time Cade returned, that hope that always shown in his eyes dimmed until there was nothing left. Nigel had taken away all his hope, all his dreams. Cade rarely slept, and when he did, it wasn't for very long.

"Yet, during those years, the three of us had formed a bond that nothing, not even Nigel, could break. We watched each other's back."

"Didn't you tell Cade about Nigel?" she asked.

"Aye. He knew."

"Why didn't he say no? Surely you could refuse an assignment."

Drogan snorted. "If it came from the king, nay. If it came from anyone else, of course. Cade refused many assignments until Nigel presented him with the ones that only came from the king."

"You knew he had forged them."

He nodded. "The three of us even confronted Nigel with it. He laughed and sent us away, but the next day he sent for Cade. I don't know what Nigel said to him, but whatever it was, Cade never refused another assignment, regardless of who it came from."

"Did Nigel send for you or Gerard like that?"

"Nay. He tried to bend us to his will, but he couldn't take away our land or titles."

She shook her head. "I don't understand why you didn't just walk away."

"We tried," Drogan confessed. "Whatever Nigel told Cade prevented him from leaving, and Gerard and I refused to leave Cade."

"But you did, didn't you?"

Drogan leaned back against the wall and briefly closed his eyes. "Nigel wanted us to do something. Gerard and I refused, but Cade had no choice. When Cade left to carry out the assignment, he never returned."

"Did you look for him?"

"Everywhere. When we couldn't find him, Gerard and I returned to our land to live in peace. Or so we thought."

Francesca inhaled deeply. "What could Nigel have told Cade to make him do whatever he wanted?"

"That's the question, isn't it?"

And one she intended to find the answer to.

Chapter Twelve

Cade welcomed the booming thunder and driving rain. He laughed as a bolt of lightning hit a tree beside him.

"Need to kill. Need to kill!"

The red haze that had fallen over his vision was gone, but the need for blood hadn't. His knives still dripped with the blood of his enemies.

And he needed more.

He glanced at Wolfglynn and thought he spotted a glimpse of fiery hair. He stilled, and his heart pounded as he squinted through the rain. Surely he had been mistaken. The downpour was too thick to see anything, but he had been sure he had glimpsed Francesca. He would have staked his life on it.

But for that moment, the need to kill diminished. It was enough and allowed him to make it to his cave without giving in to the driving hunger to slaughter everyone.

Cade stumbled into the cave, his knee connecting with a rock. He gritted his teeth and swore as pain lanced through his body. Unable to move through the pain, he took deep, slow breaths. He leaned a hand against the rocky wall of the cave. He could still smell the lingering scent of lilacs. His stomach clutched as he thought of Francesca. How he wished she was there.

"To kill her," the darkness growled.

Nay!

Cade wouldn't allow that to happen. The darkness only laughed in response.

He looked down at his hands to see them covered in blood. His tunic, breeches and boots were also stained. Bile rose in his throat. He jerked off his clothes and boots before he rushed into the storm.

Unmindful and uncaring, he dove into the churning sea. The waves pounded his body, pulling him beneath the surface until his lungs burned. He didn't fight. He wanted to die. Anything to be rid of the darkness.

"You'll never be rid of me. I'm a part of you, Cade. Now that you've unleashed me, I can take over your mind at any time."

Though he didn't want to, he found his arms clawing through the water until his head broke the surface. Cade took in several deep breaths, all the while hating what he had become.

But he had done it for Francesca and the other witches. It was a sacrifice he would gladly make again. Despite what he had become, despite the fact that it was now up to Drogan and Grayson to kill him, Cade had seen the witches safe.

The waves propelled him to shore. As Cade climbed to his feet, he walked woodenly into the cave while the darkness continued to chant its need for blood and death. Cade wasn't a fool. He was no longer in control, and when he'd had control, it was only by a slim thread. With the evil loosened, his time at Wolfglynn was up.

"Attack the castle. No one is safe from your blade. Kill all within before we move to the next village."

Cade fell to his knees, his arms outstretched as he screamed his fury.

* * * * *

Francesca's eyes flew open, her chest heaving as she gasped for breath. Though her eyes stared at the ceiling of her chamber, she didn't see it. She was reliving the dream she had of Cade. His fury and fear pulsed in her body.

She threw off the blankets and jammed her feet into her shoes. She didn't bother to change out of her nightgown. Time was of the essence, and she might already be too late.

All her years at Wolfglynn had proven beneficial, as she used back stairways and corridors that brought her out into the great hall. The hall was filled with Drogan's people seeking solace from the storm. Knights sat against walls and rested between shifts.

She had taken the back way to avoid the others. Serena and Drina would know what she was about, but she'd rather not have to try and explain. Francesca slipped through the doorway that led to the dungeons. Fortunately for her, there was no one being held, which meant no guards. She found the secret door with a sigh.

The door slid open with nary a sound. She rushed inside and ran down the dark tunnel that led to an entrance beneath the castle. She heard the sound of the waves crashing before she stumbled out of the cave, cutting her hands on the rocks.

Francesca disregarded the stinging on her palms and the rain that soaked her within moments. She was near Cade's cave. After blinking away the rain, she lifted her skirts and navigated the rocks to the cave.

The glow of a fire beckoned inside the cave. A smile pulled at her lips because she knew Cade was within. She didn't slow her steps as she entered. Just as she parted her lips to call out to Cade, cold metal touched her throat.

Francesca halted and followed the blade with her eyes until she saw Cade's hand, but the rest of him was in shadow.

"I could kill you now." His voice was low, rough, as if it weren't his own.

Dread filled Francesca, but she refused to give up. "Then do it."

He lowered the weapon and turned away. "Leave before I change my mind."

"You saved Adrianna. She and Grayson are in the castle."

Cade paused on his way to the fire. He wore only a pair of breeches.

Francesca wiped the rain from her face and followed him. "Are you wounded? Let me tend to you."

He whirled around, his lips peeled back in a snarl. "I said leave!"

She gasped as she looked into eyes of pitch. Drogan had been right. The darkness had taken over, but if that was the case, why didn't he kill her? Drogan had said Cade would need to kill and continue killing until someone stopped him.

Francesca knew that somewhere inside him, Cade was struggling with the darkness. He wouldn't give up that easily. He had fought too long and hard to give in once the darkness took over.

She lifted her hand to touch his face. His fingers wrapped around her wrist, halting her without hurting her. Undeterred, she lifted her other arm. Cade trapped that one as well.

"Don't," he said.

She shivered as a breeze filled the cave. With the wet material of her gown, chills raced over her skin. His gaze moved from her eyes to her breasts.

Her nipples were puckered and straining against the wet material. His gaze smoldered, causing her breasts to grow heavy. Dampness pooled between her legs as her blood quickened.

Francesca pulled her arms from his grasp and cupped his face. "Cade?"

"Damn you," he growled as he backed her against the wall.

Rocks dug into her back, but she felt nothing, not with Cade's heat surrounding her. He cupped her face and pressed his lips against hers. Francesca laid her palms on his bare chest. Something wicked and wanton unfurled low in her belly when he ran his tongue over her lower lip.

He lifted his head for just a moment before he took her lips in another kiss. A kiss that scorched her, made her yearn for more of him. Then he slid his tongue past her lips. Francesca sighed. His hands moved down her body to pause at her waist. He pulled her against him, pressing her breasts against his chest. A shiver of delight raced through her when she felt his hard rod pushed into her stomach.

"Witch," he murmured between kisses.

His thumbs rubbed the underside of her breasts. She moaned and tilted her head to the side as he kissed down her neck. It was only belatedly that his voice sounded more like the Cade she had come to know.

He cupped her breasts, pinching her nipples between his thumb and forefinger. Francesca gripped his shoulders as a gasp tore from her lips at the hunger that burned inside her each time Cade touched her.

She opened her eyes to find him looking at her. His eyes were more of a gray now, instead of the black. Before she could comment on it, he grasped the neck of her gown and ripped it from her body.

Her lips parted in anticipation as he looked over her body. Her breasts ached for more of his touch. The desire in his gaze made her knees weak. She had never known such hunger, such...need...before. And she wanted more.

Cade's body was on fire. For Francesca. Her kiss had been exquisite, heady as the sweetest wine. And he needed more. He needed her. Each touch and kiss sent the darkness further and further away. He knew he should send her back to the castle, back to safety. But for once, Cade was doing something for himself. The passion in her tawny eyes only propelled him onward.

His eyes traveled over her luscious body. From her full breasts tipped with pink nipples straining for his touch, to her trim waist and flared hips, to the red curls nestled between her long, lean legs, she was perfect.

In every way.

Her lips, swollen from his kisses, parted for more. He smoothed her wet locks away from her face before he buried his hand in her hair and jerked her body against his. He took her lips in a slow, sensuous kiss that told her just how much he had hungered for her, dreamed of her. He craved her so desperately that he shook with the force of his desire.

His cock jumped, eager to bury in her moist heat, to plunge into her and thrust deep again and again until she screamed his name as her body clenched around him. Only then would he allow himself to climax.

He knew he shouldn't be kissing her, much less touching her. He tempted the darkness to rise up in him, but Francesca was an allure he couldn't resist. His mouth slanted over hers again and again, drinking in her taste and her passion. Her hands clung to him, and her breathy moans would be his undoing.

When her fingers trailed down his chest to stop at the waist of his breeches, he forgot to breath. Then her hand grazed his throbbing cock, and he broke the kiss in an effort not to take her right then.

"Cade."

His name whispered on her lips only drove his desire higher. His balls tightened, and his hands shook as he cupped her breasts once again.

"By the saints, how I've wanted you," he confessed.

She smiled, then groaned when he circled a nipple with his finger.

Cade had no doubt she was untouched. She deserved better than him, better than her first time on the floor of a cave. But despite knowing that, he couldn't let her go. It wasn't just because somehow she drove the darkness away, or the way her magic made his body tingle and crave more of her touch.

It was simply because of her. The seductive tilt of her lips when she smiled, the knowledge in her tawny eyes and the call of her body to his.

Nay, Cade didn't deserve her, but he was going to take her.

Her finger unlaced his breeches, and he caught her hands in his.

"Nay," he ground out. "It's the only thing preventing me from taking you right now."

"But I want you to take me. Right now."

Cade groaned. He lifted her in his arms and walked to the fire. As soon as he set her on her feet, she retrieved one of the blankets and spread it. With a smile, she lay down on the blanket and looked at him.

If he had ever thought to turn away from her, he couldn't now. He was caught in her gaze, captured by the decadence of her body, and lulled by the taste of her lips.

Cade removed his breeches and lay down next to her. Her hand cupped his face while her thumb traced his lip, much like he had hers a day ago. He placed his hands on her stomach and felt it quiver. He couldn't remember the last time he took a woman face to face, but it was how he planned to take Francesca.

His hand caressed her hips and down her leg as he bent and kissed her neck. He worked his way down her chest until he captured a nipple in his mouth. She moaned his name, her hands threading through his hair. Her back arched as she gave him more of her breast. Cade rolled on top of her and moved to her other breasts, swirling his tongue around her nipple until she was gasping for breath, her hips grinding against him.

Her moans turned to soft cries as he continued to lave her nipples, pinching and suckling them until she was mindless with need. Only then did he kiss down her stomach to her sex. The smell of her arousal made his cock jump, and he couldn't wait to taste her. He smiled as her hands fisted in the blanket, and she watched him settle between her legs. She swallowed nervously, and he bent toward her sex.

Cade opened her women's lips with his fingers and licked her from her slit to her pearl. She cried out, her body going rigid. His tongue circled her pearl as he slid a finger inside her. She was already so wet, so hot that he didn't need to prepare her. She was ready for him.

"Cade," she cried as he sucked her pearl into his mouth.

He pushed his finger deeper, feeling the barrier that he knew he would find, and tried to ignore the voice inside that chanted she was his.

Francesca was in heaven. She had never known such bliss, such passion, and she didn't want it to stop. Cade's mouth was doing delicious things to her while his finger stroked inside her. Her hips rose of their own accord to meet his thrusts, her body knowing what was to come. She bit her lip and arched her back as something began to coil inside, tightening with each lick of his tongue and stroke of his finger.

Then he added a second finger to the first, stretching her, readying her for him. Her heart skipped a beat as she imagined him putting his cock inside her. She had felt him through his breeches, but it was nothing compared to getting to see him in all his glory. His rod was long and hard and hot as it lay against her leg.

Francesca ground her hips into his chest and moaned as his fingers increased their tempo. Whatever was building inside her was pushing her toward an edge, promising pleasure beyond her wildest dreams.

And then it claimed her.

She jerked, her body spasming with the force of her climax. Lights popped behind her eyelids as Cade continued to stroke her body, prolonging her pleasure.

Just as suddenly, he leaned over her, kissing her lips as the head of his arousal rubbed against her sensitive flesh. Francesca hissed, feeling another wave of pleasure wash over her. She watched as Cade guided himself into her; then, inch by inch, he filled her, stretching her.

"I don't want to hurt you," he said with his eyes closed.

Francesca smiled and brought his face down for another kiss. "My body is yours. Take it."

His eyes opened, and she saw they were a light gray now. He pulled out of her only to plunge further inside, pushing past her maidenhead. She stiffened, feeling an instant of pain, yet it faded as quickly as it had begun.

As soon as Cade began to move again, the wonderful passion swirling inside her intensified. She wrapped her legs around his waist and met his thrusts. He alternated between long, slow thrusts and hard and fast ones, and each sent her building toward another orgasm.

Each time he drove into her, he rubbed against her aching pearl, bringing her closer and closer until she screamed his name as her second climax hit. Francesca felt Cade stiffen over her and opened her eyes to find his head thrown back, a look of joy on his face as his seed spilled inside her womb.

Chapter Thirteen

Cade had never felt such...peace...in all his days. He gazed down to find Francesca looking at him with an expression of such delight that it made his heart catch.

He bent and kissed her lips, still amazed that she had wanted him, despite the darkness. He pulled out of her and wet a piece of material to wipe her virgin's blood from between her leg and on his cock. Once they were clean, he rolled onto his back, pulling her against him so that her head rested on his chest.

"You're eyes are blue again," she said.

He hadn't known they had changed. "What color where they before?"

"Black. Then they turned to gray, and now blue."

He knew they had changed because of her. Somehow, whether it was Francesca herself or her magic, she had driven the darkness away. For the time being.

"Are you all right?"

He looked down at her and nodded. "Better than I've been in a very long time."

"So all you needed was a woman?" The teasing note in her voice brought a grin to his lips.

"Nay. All I needed was you."

Her gaze lowered for a moment. "What happened?"

"You mean with Nigel's army?"

She nodded and shifted so that she rested her chin on her hand, which lay on his chest.

"I had only one choice that would get Grayson and Adrianna to the castle."

"Hmm. That was very brave of you. You fought the darkness for so long, and then finally gave in. What did it feel like?"

"Hell," he answered without hesitation. "Like I had no control over myself. One moment I was standing before the army, and the next, they were scattered on the ground. Yet my thirst for blood only increased."

She sighed. "That's what Drogan said would happen to you. How did you beat it?"

"I didn't. At least not alone."

"What do you mean?"

"I tried to drown in the sea," he confessed. "I wanted to die. It was better than having the evil urge me to attack Wolfglynn and kill all within it. Yet the darkness wouldn't let me drown. Even when I climbed out of the water, it hungered for death and destruction."

Francesca's eyes held sorrow and compassion, but not pity as she listened to him. "Yet you fought it."

"I tried. I could've killed you."

"But you didn't. Don't question it. Just be glad you were able to win against it."

He sighed. "For now."

He'd let it out, unleashed it. How much longer did he have before the red haze of blood descended on him again?

She kissed his chest, above his nipple.

"Why did you come?"

She shrugged. "I had a dream about you."

"A dream?"

"It is my gift as a *bana-bhuidseach*. Serena sees how people will die. Adrianna is a healer, and she can see danger approaching her. Grayson can heal himself."

"What?" Cade asked, interrupting her.

Francesca smiled. "Aye. It appears he is also a witch. It's been centuries since our kind has had a male with magic."

"I don't understand."

"The *bana-bhuidseach* are a dying race of witches, cursed by one of our own."

"Tell me," he urged.

She rolled onto her back, the firelight licking at her skin, stirring his desire. "There isn't much to tell. Through time and the retelling, we lost the truth of where our kind came from before England. Some say we came from a land of sand and sun, a land with monuments that reached the sky."

Cade rolled onto his side, his head supported by his hand. "What happened?"

"We lived in peace with the others of this land. Every *bana-bhuidseach* had magic, both male and female. Instead of living in small groups, we chose to live in one large city."

He watched the play of emotions on her face as she retold her story. It made her sad, but he also saw a spark of anger in her tawny depths.

"One of the village elders who held everyone together had a son who fell in love with Helen. It is said that Helen was the most beautiful woman to ever walk the earth. She was perfect in every way, not a flaw on her body."

Cade could argue that Francesca was the most beautiful woman, but he held silent and let her finish.

"Helen also claimed to fall in love with the son. Preparations for the wedding began immediately. Then, one day, a man came into the city. He wasn't one of us. However, he was of noble blood, with lots of coin and a large castle. Helen decided she'd rather be with the noble and ran off with him.

"The son was so depressed that the love of his life had left him that he threw himself into the river and drowned. The village elder grieved for the loss of her son, and in her pain, she cursed Helen."

"What was the curse?"

Francesca let out a long breath. "That Helen's noble would leave her within three months after she bore him a child."

"Did he?"

"I don't know."

Cade frowned. "The woman cursed Helen, so how did it affect all of you?"

"In her anger, she cursed all of the *bana-bhuidseach* women. She tried to reverse it later, but it was too late. The damage had been done."

Cade drummed his fingers on the blanket. "The curse can't have worked. Drogan is still with Serena, and it's been more than three months since she had given him a child."

"Apparently, Serena broke the curse for herself. I think Adrianna has as well. Grayson's parents were both witches, though he never knew it until recently."

"Your father?"

She licked her lips. "He was killed in battle three months to the day of my birth."

"By all that's holy."

"It's why we're dying out."

Cade caught her gaze. "Is that why you've never married?"

"Would you? Knowing that your wife would die or leave you within three months of giving you a child?"

"Serena and Drogan took the chance."

Francesca turned and looked out the cave. "How long do you think the storm will go on?"

Cade let her change the subject. "I've angered Nigel. It could go on for days."

He lifted a lock of her hair, loving the color and silken texture. There had been nothing he'd ever done in his life that let him deserve Francesca.

She turned her head toward him and rolled onto her side so they were facing each other. "You left Nigel, didn't you?"

Drogan had asked him that question a thousand times, and he'd never answered. He hadn't wanted to before. Now, he did. "Aye."

She reached out with her hand and entwined her fingers with his.

"Drogan said you came to their group with hope in your eyes. You must have had big dreams."

"What does any boy dream of but honor and glory?"

"Will you tell me how you came to be with Drogan and Gerard?"

For a moment he thought about telling her no, but then decided it couldn't hurt. "It was the king himself who saw me at a tournament. He asked that I join his royal guard."

"What an honor," she said with awe in her voice.

"I thought so. My father had died the previous year, and I was in charge of everything. Going with the king was the glory I had always dreamed of."

"Did you have other family? A mother? Sisters? Brothers perhaps?"

Cade's chest tightened just remembering his family. "Aye," was all he answered. "I was young, the youngest actually, to ever be in the royal guard. My skill with weapons is what also caught Nigel's eye. When he asked me to join an elite group of men that served the king, I didn't hesitate."

"Drogan and Gerard."

He nodded. "They weren't too much older than me, but if you looked in their eyes, it seemed they were ancient."

"Did that worry you?"

"It should've, but being so young, I thought I was invincible. Drogan and Gerard brought me into the fold. The bond we formed then is unbreakable to this day."

"I asked Drogan what happened with Nigel."

Cade stiffened. It was the one thing he didn't want her to know. Well, it was one of the things he didn't want her to know.

"He told me it was your story to tell," she said.

Cade let out a breath.

"Is it so terrible that you don't want me to know?"

"Aye," he murmured.

"Drogan told me you were assassins for the king. I can imagine what you were sent to do."

He lowered his gaze to her lips. If she knew, really knew what he had done, she wouldn't be with him now. "Nay, you can't imagine, witch."

Her fingernail ran lightly over his skin from his shoulder to his hip. "Then tell me."

"I cannot."

"Why didn't you return to Drogan and Gerard? They searched for you."

Cade swallowed and met her gaze. "Because the darkness had taken hold of me."

"It had taken a hold of Gerard and Drogan as well."

"Nay. They had it, aye, but it was nothing like what was in me. I feared being around anyone. I tried to outrun it, but the evil was always there. Nigel was always there."

She cupped his cheek and smiled. "Yet you were able to get away from Nigel. So did Gerard and Drogan."

"The only reason he let Gerard and Drogan go for as long as he did was because he knew I would return to protect them. Attacking Drogan the first time was Nigel's way of finding me."

She paused, wariness in her gaze. "Are you sure?"

"Positive."

"Does Drogan know?"

Cade shrugged one shoulder. "I doubt it. It doesn't matter. Nigel is coming back regardless."

"For you or for Drogan?"

"For me. He'd attack Drogan just to get me here."

Francesca licked her lips. "What did you do that made him hate you so much?"

"It's not what I did, witch, but what I am. If he captures me, I will be but a pawn for him. He'll rule the darkness through me."

"Saints," she whispered.

Cade lifted a brow at her idea of cursing. "I won't let him capture me."

"How are you going to stop him? Nigel is powerful enough to rule the weather. What else can he do?"

Cade almost smiled as he watched the fire in her eyes. She was lovely when she was riled, and the thought of Nigel winning sent her tawny eyes dancing with ire.

"What is Nigel capable of?" she asked again.

But Cade didn't want to talk about Nigel or the hideous acts he could conjure up since selling his soul to the devil. He wanted more of Francesca, wanted more of her hands and lips on his skin. But more than that, he wanted to be inside her again.

Cade placed his hand on her back and pulled her toward him. Her eyes widened when she felt his hard cock between them. He burned for another taste of her, to hear her cries of pleasure.

Her hand moved between them and gripped his rod. Cade hissed in a breath, feeling her soft fingers closed around him. He closed his eyes as his blood fired his veins, demanding that he sink into her heat.

"Do you like that?" Francesca asked.

"Too much."

"I want to explore you as you've explored me."

Cade was about to spill just from the inexperienced touch of her hand. If he let her lick and kiss him as she had done her, he wouldn't last a heartbeat.

"Not this time." He grasped her and rolled her with him as he shifted onto his back.

With her legs straddling his hips, she rotated her damp sex against him. "I like this."

Cade groaned. Her hair had begun to dry in damp waves of red that cascaded down her back to tease his legs. He sat up and plunged his hands into her hair as he took her mouth in a fierce, needful kiss.

She moaned into his mouth, her nails scraping his back as he deepened the kiss. He reached between them and teased her nipples with his fingers, pinching the tiny buds until her hips rocked against him.

"Easy, witch," he murmured into her ear before he took the lobe into his mouth and suckled.

"Cade, please. I need you."

His balls tightened at her words. He most assuredly didn't deserve his witch, but he would have her as long as he was able.

His witch.

Aye, she's mine.

Cade had never felt so possessive of a woman before, never wanted to cling to hope and a future he had dreamed of so many years ago. But Francesca made him think it could all be possible again.

He knew it wasn't, but she gave him the kernel of hope he hadn't had in so very long.

He grasped Francesca by her waist and lifted her until her sex hovered over his raging cock. Instinctively, he knew she would be the only woman who could calm the darkness.

Her tawny gaze met his, a seductive smile on her swollen lips. "Please."

Slowly, he lowered her. She was wet and slid easily over his length until he was seated to the root. Cade wrapped his arms around her and slanted his mouth over hers for another kiss.

When her arms wound around his neck, he began to rock her hips back and forth with his hands. She gasped and dropped her head back, her lips parted on a moan. Cade had never seen anything so alluring, so erotic in his entire life.

He shifted, and it took him deeper within her. She moaned his name, her nails sinking into his shoulder, and she took over the rocking motion.

"Put the soles of your feet together," he told her. "Then, use your legs to ride me."

She bit her bottom lip as she did as he instructed. The first time she moved, Cade groaned low in his throat. With her heat and tight channel around him, he wouldn't last long. When she quickened her pace, he knew she wasn't long in peaking. He cupped her head and looked into her eyes. He wanted to see her as she came, wanted to experience a closeness with this witch.

"Cade," she whispered before she clenched around him.

The feel of her tightening around his cock sent him over the edge. Cade stiffened and shuddered as he climaxed, his gaze locked with Francesca's.

And for a the barest of moments, he thought he saw the future. A future with him and his witch.

Chapter Fourteen

Cade opened his eyes to find the fire dying. He wasn't sure when he'd fallen asleep, but with Francesca snuggled against him, it had been the best rest he'd had since he'd joined the king's Royal Guard.

Anyone, or anything, could have snuck up on him, and he wouldn't have known it. That frightened Cade much more than he wanted.

He gradually extracted his arm from beneath the witch and rose to add logs to the fire. With the rain, it was damp and cool in the cave, and he didn't want Francesca to get sick. Once the fire was blazing, he turned to get another blanket. A heartbeat after he placed the blanket over her, he paused, the hairs on the back of his neck standing on end.

Cade jerked on his breeches and grasped his knives. He moved to the shadows of the cave near the entrance and waited. Just moments later, a shape moved to enter, much as Francesca had done earlier.

He brought his blade to the intruder's throat.

"Is this how you treat a friend?"

Cade cursed and lowered his weapon as he recognized Drogan's voice. "Get out."

"Not until I know what you did to Francesca."

"The witch is fine."

"I want to see her," Drogan argued, his gold eyes hard.

Cade gripped his knives. He didn't want anyone looking at his witch. "I said she's fine."

Drogan took a step toward him. "If you've harmed her...."

"What will you do? Kill me as I asked you to do so long ago?"

"Cade," Drogan growled.

"The witch is fine," Cade said again. "She's by the fire."

Drogan looked over Cade's shoulder. Unable to help himself, Cade turned to look at his witch. A slender arm had come out of the blanket. Anger burned within him as he realized Drogan had seen her.

When he turned around, Drogan's gaze had changed—a look of uncertainty and...optimism flared. "Do you care for her?"

"Stop looking at her," Cade said between clenched teeth.

Drogan held up his hands and turned so that his back was to Francesca. "Answer me, Cade. Do you care for her?"

"She touches me as no one has."

Drogan's looked at him. "The darkness claimed you, didn't it?"

Cade gave a small jerk of his head.

"And Francesca soothed you?"

"She gave me peace," he admitted. "Peace that I haven't known in years."

Drogan blew out a breath. "You came back from the darkness. It's almost impossible to believe. What was it like?"

"You don't want to know."

"Yet you didn't harm Fran."

Cade shook his head. "I couldn't. Despite what the darkness wanted, I couldn't hurt her."

"Does it still have a hold on you?"

"Not at the moment."

Drogan rubbed his chin, a worried expression furrowing his brow. "Cade, as much as I'm happy that you've found some peace, I have concerns about Fran."

"You mean because of the curse, or because you two grew up like brother and sister?"

"Both, I guess," he confessed. "Fran has always kept herself closed off from everyone, including my uncle, whom she considers a father."

"I know she needs to stay away from me," Cade said. "I know it, yet I can't imagine never seeing her again. Nigel is coming, and I've never known such fear, such rage as I do when I think of him touching her."

"I know."

Cade glanced at the man he had called brother. "There is no future for the witch and me. I plan on killing Nigel."

Drogan turned towards him, but Cade held up a hand. "I know what you would say, and I thank you for it. I don't know what would have become of me if you and Gerard hadn't been there. I owe you both so much. Ending Nigel is the least I can do."

As much as Cade had missed talking to Drogan, all he wanted now was for his friend to leave so he could return to Francesca. He wanted to lie beside her, to feel her soft curves press against him, to have her warm breath fan his skin as she slept.

He wanted her.

"What happens now?"

Cade shrugged. "I don't know. We wait. I've raised Nigel's ire. He could send another army, he could send another wolf, or he could come himself."

"The river has begun to rise over the banks from all the rain."

Cade let that information sink in. "Have you gathered all your people inside the castle walls?"

"Not all. I plan on collecting them on the morrow. Some are near the river and could be flooded."

"Don't go yourself," Cade cautioned. "You never know what Nigel has planned."

Drogan crossed his arms over his chest and raised an auburn brow. "I am lord here, Cade. I will see to my people."

"So I'm wasting my time trying to protect you? Nigel let you and Gerard go because he planned to use both of you as bait for me. Don't make this harder than it is."

"Are you saying all these years when I thought I was done with Nigel, he was merely playing with me? Teasing me with freedom?"

Cade reluctantly nodded.

"You need to leave here," Drogan said as he dropped his arms and ran a hand down his face. "Leave. Return to your home and see your family. Ready your own castle. If you're right and Nigel wants you, he'll leave me alone."

Cade didn't respond. How could he, when he knew there was nothing left of his ancestral home? Sure, the stones still stood, at least a majority of them did. His tenants, his people, for the most part had stayed and continued to work the land.

He'd ensured that he had a trustworthy steward to see to everything for the next lord of Stonelake. Cade had no intentions of ever returning. He had nothing to return for.

"Cade."

He blinked and glanced at Drogan to see his brows drawn together, his voice harsh as if he had called to him many times. "Aye?"

"My castle is protected with the witches' magic. I'll be fine. See to your own people."

Cade nodded, knowing Drogan wouldn't stop arguing the point unless he thought Cade had agreed.

"Good," Drogan said with a sigh. "Now, I must return to my wife. She's worried sick over Francesca."

Cade waited until Drogan disappeared in the rain before he turned back to his witch. Francesca had rolled onto her side to face him, the blanket dipping down so that one pink nipple was visible.

95

He hardened instantly. He feared after his taste of her, he would never get enough. Already the thought of her leaving, even if it was only to the castle for more clothes, left him in a cold sweat.

Her tale of the curse was interesting. He had never given much credence to curses. He believed that the more a person gave stock to the curse, the more power the curse held over you. Husbands died and left. That was the way of the world.

That it happened within three months of the birth of the children seemed odd, but he was sure not all the witches had been spoken with after their husbands left or died to refute the curse. But Francesca believed in the curse. And by the protective light in Drogan's eyes, so did he.

Cade removed his breeches and lifted the blanket lay behind Fran, his body molded hers. He let his arm fall over her waist as he brought her against him. She made a soft mewling sound in her sleep and burrowed closer to him.

Unable to stop his thoughts, he found himself drifting through memories of his home. Stonelake was picturesque, quiet, and fed his soul. He'd been loath to leave it and his family, but the prospect of honor and glory had been too much of a temptation. Had he known that accepting Nigel's offer as an assassin would prevent him from ever returning, Cade would never have taken it.

Drogan and Gerard had tried to warn him, had cautioned him about believing Nigel. But Cade had been naïve. Nigel's silver tongue had told Cade exactly what he wanted to hear, and Cade had no way of knowing that Nigel was putting evil into his soul.

If he'd met Francesca before now, before Nigel could sink his claws into him, maybe he would have been able to see what Nigel was about.

The future Cade had always dreamed of, with a castle full of children and a wife who stood by his side, had disappeared long ago. Or so he thought. Being near Francesca made him think of those long ago hopes and dreams.

Cade's family had a good name and plenty of coin. He would have been a good catch for any noble family.

His eyes closed when he thought of his father. His father had been a wise, patient man, a man who had instilled in Cade the need for family and honor. Cade had wanted to make him proud. Proud was the last thing his father would be now, looking down from heaven.

Cade wouldn't even be able to see his family, because once he died, he knew his soul was bound for Hell. Especially after what he had done to his mother and sisters.

His heart began to race, and he broke out into a cold sweat every time he thought of that dark day. Cade buried his face in Francesca's hair and inhaled the fragrance of lilacs.

Almost instantly, he felt a calm descend over him. Was it Francesca's magic, or the woman herself? Somehow, some way, she held sway over Cade's soul as no one else, not even Nigel, had been able to.

* * * * *

"Well?" Serena demanded when Drogan walked into their chamber.

He shook his head rapidly, and water went everywhere. Only after he had removed his wet clothing and climbed into bed beside her did he let out a loud sigh.

Serena drummed her fingers as she watched her husband lie back with his hands behind his head and his gaze on the canopy above them.

"Drogan," she urged.

"She's with Cade," he finally answered.

Serena paused, her heart lurching. "I knew it. I know you're glad for Cade, but...."

"You wonder about Fran."

"Aye," she nodded. She turned onto her side and touched her husband's arm. "If she's with Cade, does that mean the darkness hadn't taken him as we feared?"

Drogan's gold eyes met hers. "That's just it, love. It had taken him."

"I don't understand. You told me once it takes hold of him, he's lost."

"So I thought. It seems that Fran has the power to rid Cade of the darkness. He told me the evil wanted him to kill her, urged him to do it. But he couldn't."

"Oh." Serena thought over his words for a moment. "Did you see Fran? Is she all right?"

He nodded. "I saw her, though I didn't speak to her."

"Why?"

"Cade nearly ripped my head from my body every time I looked at her, and as to why, she was asleep. Naked under the blanket."

Serena fell back on her pillow. "Oh."

"Precisely."

"She calmed him?"

"Brought him peace, he said. The few times I've glimpsed Cade since he left Gerard and me, his gaze was haunted. Yet, tonight, he did appear at peace. Not quite the boy I first met with such grand hopes and dreams, but a man who knew what he'd done and was planning a future."

Serena moved to lay her head on Drogan's chest, his hand absently caressing her bare back. "I've always gotten the sense from Fran that she doesn't plan to have a future."

"Cade said they didn't have a future, that he planned to kill Nigel, which would in turn kill him."

"Fran isn't going to like that."

Drogan's shoulder moved in a shrug. "Maybe she knows."

"She's been here every day, no matter the weather, ever since Nigel's last attack. She's fortified the castle with magic, and I've even seen her in the armory protecting those weapons."

"She just wants to make sure we're protected."

Serena let out a breath. "Maybe. Yet, I could easily have protected the castle and weapons with my magic, and I have. I just feel...I don't know, that maybe she's hiding something from us."

"Her power is dreams. Do you think she saw something?"

"Nay. If she had, she would tell us. I'm sure of it."

"Then what?"

Serena caressed his abdomen. "I tried to see her death the other day. She didn't even know I had done it, she was so preoccupied in looking for Cade."

"What did you see?"

"I couldn't."

He shifted so that he leaned on his elbow and stared down at her. "You couldn't?"

"There was nothing but never ending blackness."

"Death is something that comes to us all, love. Don't look again. It always hurts your soft heart, and I cannot stand to see you upset."

Serena smiled. It still surprised her that she had beaten the curse, that she not only had her son, but she had Drogan. A strong, powerful man who gave love like she had only dreamed about.

"I know," she admitted. "I just had to look. Fran seems different lately, almost like she's closing herself off."

"She's always been like that. You've only known her a little over a year, love. I've known her nearly my entire life. Though I was gone a lot from Wolfglynn, Phineas wrote me often. He was ever worried about Francesca."

"I would never have thought she would be interested in Cade."

Drogan gathered her into his arms and kissed her forehead. "No one knows what the future holds. All we can do is hope for the best. As for Cade and Fran, I didn't expect it either, but I'm happy for both of them. They were both alone. Now they have each other."

Serena snuggled against him. Drogan was right, but she couldn't stop worrying. For Fran, for Cade, for everyone. Evil was coming, and it intended to kill them all.

Chapter Fifteen

Francesca came awake slowly, her body sated in a way she had never experienced before. She smiled as images of Cade flashed in her mind. She opened her eyes to find the rain had begun to slow, which made her sad.

She wasn't ready to leave Cade. Not now, possibly not ever. Even when she'd had the new dream about Nigel, it hadn't frightened her as it had in past nights, because she'd been in Cade's arms.

One of his arms was beneath her head, and her back was pressed against his side. She rolled over, surprised to find him still asleep. He had said he rarely slept, yet to look at him now, he looked serene and almost boyish.

The fire had all but died, though the coals still glowed. The sun tried to break through the thick clouds of the storm, which gave her enough light in which to see Cade.

She ran her finger down his cheek, the stubble of his beard scratching her skin. Her gaze raked freely over his body. She marveled at his sculpted muscles, the strength of body and mind evident just by looking at him.

Her hand skimmed his chest and over his flat belly to the line of golden hair that ran to his flaccid rod. He had kicked the blanket off one leg that was dusted with more of his golden hair.

She felt the soreness betwixt her legs and smiled. Cade had touched her as no other man ever had, but he'd done more than make love to her. She had opened herself fully to him, given everything.

And in return, she had seen a part of him she hadn't expected.

For just a moment last night, as they had made love and he'd held her gaze, she had glimpsed the boy he once was. It had stirred her heart. And when he'd asked about the curse, she hadn't hesitated in telling him. Which was odd. She never spoke of it. It wasn't as if she tried to ignore it—she just didn't want to think of it.

Yet, after speaking of it to Cade, after witnessing him accept what she said as real, she had felt good. Maybe it was his expert hands and the way he made love to her, maybe it was because she leaned upon Cade instead of keeping her problems to herself. Whatever the reason, she never wanted the feelings to end. Never.

Her hand stopped just short of touching his cock. Last night, he had been incredibly rigid, thrusting hard and deep inside her.

She circled the tip of his rod before she placed her hand over him. To her surprise, he began to harden before her eyes. Francesca's breath came faster, moisture gathering between her legs as she felt his heat.

Unable to help herself, she wrapped her fingers around him. She hadn't expected him to be so soft, so hot.

"By the saints, witch," Cade said, his voice gruff from sleep as his gaze pinned hers.

She grinned as she slowly moved her hand up and down his length. When he said "witch," it sounded like an endearment, and she loved it. "I cannot help myself when it comes to you."

"You're sore. We shouldn't."

But the desire in his vivid blue gaze told her he wanted her as much as she did him. Francesca decided words would be useless. Action was needed instead. Remembering how he had licked her sex, making her mindless with need, she lowered her head and traced the swollen head of his arousal with her tongue.

He hissed in a breath, his hands threading into her hair. She worried that he might try to force her head up, but instead, his hands seemed to hold her there, almost as if he were afraid she would stop.

Francesca grew bolder with each stroke of her tongue. She slid her lips over his head and took his rod in her mouth. Up and down her head moved, taking him deeper in her mouth each time. His groans drove her wild, urging her to give him more pleasure.

He began to move his hips, to thrust upward each time she took him in her mouth. And when his hands moved between her legs to caress her, she jerked at the pleasure, her moans joining his.

She cupped his balls, rolling them gently in her hands. He groaned and thrust two fingers inside her. Francesca closed her eyes as the sensations engulfed her. The next heartbeat, she was on her back and Cade between her legs. He lifted her leg and plunged inside her.

Francesca gasped at the sensation of him filling her. He held still for a moment, their gazes locking. Her heart skipped a beat as she looked into his blue eyes. Her feelings for Cade had grown quickly in the past few days, and she feared she was falling in love with him.

Would it be so bad to give my heart to such a brave man?

The answer was nay, but having to leave him would be impossible. And she had no choice in that matter.

"Witch?" he asked, concern in his eyes.

She cupped his face. "I'm overwhelmed with the pleasure you give me. Don't stop."

For a moment, she didn't think he would accept her excuse, but then he began to move within her. She forgot about everything and everyone save the man who had shown her paradise.

Francesca arched her back as he scraped her nipple lightly with his teeth before suckling the tiny bud. He plunged into her with long, slow strokes that sent her body wild with desire. She couldn't get enough of him, couldn't get close enough to him.

Her body began the familiar tightening that happened when she was about to climax. She wasn't ready, didn't want to stop the desire being with Cade gave her. But her body didn't listen.

When he quickened his pace, their bodies slapping against each other and sweat glistening on their skin, she was powerless to stop the orgasm. She gripped his shoulders as wave upon wave of bliss washed over her, sending her spiraling down an abyss.

With her body still pulsing from the power of her climax, she opened her eyes to see Cade's body jerk and shudder as his own orgasm took hold. He buried his head in her neck and held her while his cock jumped inside her, filling her with his seed.

Knowing any day Nigel would arrive, signaling her death, Francesca should have been frightened of getting with child. Yet the thought of Cade's child growing inside her filled her with a warmth she hadn't expected.

She had never wanted children. Not until now.

"Witch," he murmured as he kissed her neck, her cheek, her eyelids, the tip of her nose, and then her mouth.

Francesca wrapped her arms around his neck, ignoring the fact that the rain had stopped. She didn't want to leave. There would be questions that she didn't want to answer, but it wasn't that. She didn't want to leave Cade.

He rolled off her and sighed. After a moment he rose, pulled on his breeches, and built up the fire. Francesca wrapped the blanket around her against the cool morning sea breeze. She smiled when he brought her some oatcakes and a water skin. They ate their morning meal in silence, each lost in thought.

Finally, Francesca broke the silence. "I'm not ready for this to end."

"But it has to," he said and met her eyes over the fire. "For your safety, you must get to the castle and stay there."

"And you? You'll walk the forest until Nigel arrives?"

"Aye."

Tears stung her eyes. "I won't see you again, will I?"

"Don't think I'm sending you to the castle because I don't want you, witch. I'm doing it because I can't stand the thought of you getting hurt."

"What of you?" she argued. "How do you think I feel standing in the castle? Alone. Wondering if you're all right, if Nigel has already found and killed you."

Cade sighed and shifted his gaze to the fire. "I won't survive Nigel's attack. I've known this from the beginning. I'm going to kill Nigel, which will kill the darkness within me."

"And in doing so, kill you," she finished.

He met her gaze. "The darkness is a part of me now. There is no separating it, as much as I wish it otherwise. Nigel needs to die. I need to die lest the darkness take over again."

"You beat it last night."

"Only because of you. I don't know why, and I'm not going to try to understand. Maybe it's your magic."

She shook her head. "Does Drogan know you plan to die?"

"Aye. I told him last night."

Francesca stiffened. "You left me?"

"Drogan came here looking for you. He was worried that I might have hurt you. Once he realized you were safe, he left."

"But not before you told him your plans."

Cade nodded. "Everyone needs to stay in the castle. That includes you. I've planned too hard and too long for this to go awry."

"You're not going to let anyone help you, are you?"

"No one can help me, witch. I'm the only one who can kill Nigel."

She didn't argue, even though she knew for a fact he was wrong. So very wrong. And she was going to make sure he knew that in the end.

Francesca finished her oatcake and rose to her feet. She bit back a wince at the pull between her legs. Her nightgown was useless, having been ripped in two. She wasn't sure how she would get back into the castle without being seen, especially since it was already dawn.

"The storm has stopped," she said as she walked to the entrance.

"He's on his way."

She glanced at Cade, surprised to find him beside her. She hadn't heard him move. "Can you feel him?"

"Aye."

"And the darkness? Is it still there?"

He turned his head to look at her. "You calmed it, witch, but it's still there. It'll try to rise again soon."

"Let me stay and help you."

One side of his mouth lifted in a sad smile. "What kind of knight and lord would I be if I allowed you to stay and put your life in danger?"

"The kind who wanted to be rid of the evil inside him."

He cupped her face, his thumbs caressing her bottom lip. "You are the bravest woman I know."

She knew it was useless to argue. He was only trying to protect her. She would leave, but she would also come back. "I'd better return now, since I'm not properly dressed."

"Wait." He walked toward the back of the cave and reappeared with a long cloak. "It's not a gown, but it'll be better than a blanket."

Francesca wrapped the cloak around her and held it in place with her hands. She would have to take small steps in order to keep her bare legs from showing.

"Be safe, witch," he said as he bent to kiss her softly, and all too quickly.

She stopped herself from pulling his head back down for another kiss. She would not beg. "You as well."

With that, she turned and started toward the castle.

Cade felt as though someone ripped his heart out. It had taken everything he had to send Francesca away. Already he missed her, her scent, her magic. It wouldn't be long now before the darkness tried to take over again. It had tasted power, and it wouldn't be satisfied until it had it.

He jerked off his breeches and grabbed a bar of soap as he strode to the water. The waves were like ice slamming into his legs, but still he waded deeper and deeper. The cold water cooled the desire boiling his blood, which was what he needed to keep away from Francesca.

After lathering the bar, he scrubbed his body and hair before he rinsed and swam back to shore. He rubbed his jaw and felt the prick of his whiskers. He'd never liked the feel of a beard on his face. After he pulled on his breeches and boots, he reached for his dagger and set about shaving.

His mind wandered, thinking of his family and Stonelake. He wondered if his land was a beautiful as it used to be. Francesca would love it, he was sure of it. He wished he could show it to her.

Fool.

He was a fool. Death was coming. There was no future for him, no hope of evading Hell, no hope of having Francesca forever.

He had set his fate in motion by accepting Nigel's offer. Nigel brought death and blood wherever he went. Cade had feared him greatly in the beginning, and when Nigel had threatened his mother, brother and sisters, Cade had given in to his demands.

Had Nigel known then that the darkness, when it first took hold and was uncontrollable, would lead him to kill his family? Had he laughed when he'd learned the news?

Cade squeezed his eyes shut as he recalled his sister's frightened face staring up at him, begging him not to kill her. He had tried to get control from the darkness, tried to stop. But he hadn't been able to.

It had been his fault for going back to Stonelake to begin with. But he had needed his family. If only he'd known how powerful the darkness was.

He shuddered and tried to push their deaths from his mind. He could blame it on the darkness all he wanted, but the truth was he was a murderer. He had killed everyone in his family, leaving the castle coated with blood.

But it had been Nigel who'd set it on fire.

Chapter Sixteen

Francesca walked the back corridors of the castle, much as she had done hours before when she'd left to seek out Cade. Her dream had made her leave the castle, but she knew she would have gone to see him anyway.

When the door to her chamber closed behind her, she leaned against it and closed her eyes, remembering Cade's hands, his mouth. She shivered and removed his cloak. A servant had already been inside her chamber to get her morning bath ready.

The water was still hot when Francesca slid into the wooden tub. Normally, she relaxed and got her mind together for the day, but this morning was different. This morning, action was needed.

Francesca hurriedly washed before drying off and reaching for the cream gown that was her favorite. The elongated sleeves, neckline and hem were adorned with thread of burnished gold. Once she was dressed, she combed out her hair and braided it.

She needed to talk to Drogan. The men most likely had a plan, and though she had no intentions of telling them everything, she could aid them in the battle.

Francesca found everyone in the great hall breaking their morning fast. Drogan smiled at her and motioned for her to sit. Though she normally sat at the dais with them, she needed to be able to see everyone, so she chose to sit at another table.

"Did you sleep well?" he asked.

Grayson looked up at Drogan's question, but Fran kept her eyes on Drogan. "I did."

"The storm has passed," Adrianna said. "I don't sense another."

"Nigel is controlling the storms, so one could hit any time," Serena said. "We need to be prepared."

Drogan nodded. "I'm going to see how much damage there is. I suspect there is flooding with the river."

"And the lightning," Serena added.

Drogan grunted in response. "Grayson, will you ride with me?"

"Aye," Grayson said around a mouthful of food.

Francesca took a deep breath and pushed her food around her trencher. "Cade will be angry that you're leaving the castle."

"I know," Drogan said. "I need to see to my people, though."

"She has a point," Adrianna said. "He risked his very soul for us. The least we could do would be to stay safe."

"No one is safe from Nigel," Drogan ground out, his voice growing louder with each word. "No one. Do you think I like sitting in my safe castle while my people, my brother are out there fighting alone?"

"We cannot let him die," Francesca said. All eyes turned to her. She licked her lips and folded her hands in her lap as she sifted in her seat to face them. "Cade plans to kill Nigel himself. He believes that the evil inside him will die with Nigel, but it will also kill Cade."

"Shite," Grayson said and shoved his trencher away from him. "You spoke with Cade? Again?"

"Last night," Drogan answered for her. "We both spoke with him, though I believe he told her more."

Adrianna looked from Francesca to Drogan. "There is more going on here than we're being told."

Francesca knew they would all learn the truth soon enough. She didn't like lies anyway, and she carried a big enough secret without adding another. "I was with Cade. All night."

"I see," Adrianna said with a knowing look.

Serena smiled. "You've found happiness, Fran. It's what we've wanted for you for a long time."

Francesca glanced at her hands. "Cade didn't tell me all his plans, but I do know he believes Nigel will attack any day."

"Any day?" Adrianna asked.

Grayson took her hands in his. "It'll be fine, Drina. I'll protect you."

"It won't be alright," Francesca said as she got to her feet. "I've seen it. In my dreams. The devastation is...catastrophic."

"Why haven't you told me before?" Drogan demanded as he leaned forward and rested his forearms on the table.

"Why do you think I've been placing every ounce of magic I can into this castle? Why do you think I've begged you to stay within its walls?" she countered.

Serena rose and walked around the dais to take Francesca's hands. "How long have you known?"

"Since I was ten summers."

Adrianna sucked in a breath, Grayson let out a string of curses, and Drogan raked a hand through his hair.

"You should have said something," Drogan said. "That is information I needed to know."

Fran raised a brow. "Its information you have that Cade doesn't. I tell you now, because"—she paused, her stomach fluttering—"Cade needs to be saved, too."

"I don't know that he can be," Grayson said.

Serena rolled her eyes. "Cade had been overtaken by the darkness yesterday, just as we all feared."

"But," Adrianna said, her eyes wide, "He didn't harm Fran or Drogan."

Drogan fisted his hands on the table as if he were struggling to contain his frustration over the situation. "Cade told me that somehow Fran pushed away the darkness, gave him peace, if you will. Maybe it's her magic."

"Nay," Serena and Adrianna said in unison.

Francesca looked from one to the other. "If it's not my magic, then what is it?"

"Your heart," Serena answered softly.

She already knew that she cared for Cade much more than she should, and though she thought she might be falling in love with him, Fran wasn't sure and wouldn't admit it.

"Cade cares for her," Drogan said, unaware of her turmoil. "He's very protective."

"Love?" Grayson asked.

Drogan shrugged. "Maybe."

"Enough," Francesca said. "This isn't about my feelings for Cade, or his feelings for me. This is about keeping everyone alive. Even Cade."

"I'm not sure that we can," Adrianna said. "Doesn't Cade believe he's the only one who can battle Nigel?"

Francesca's heart pounded in her ears. She wanted to tell them, to assure them that she could battle Nigel and win, but she knew neither Drogan nor Grayson would allow her out of the castle. And if Cade ever learned what she planned, he would likely tie her to her bed to keep her away from Nigel. Nay, it was better to keep that secret to herself.

"Aye," Serena said. "Cade has the best chance at winning."

Adrianna gained her feet and walked to stand on Francesca's other side. "We're *bana-bhuidseach*. Combined, our magic can heal him, and we will make sure he doesn't die."

Francesca smiled, but as she turned away, she caught Drogan watching her intently. If she wasn't careful, he would figure out she was hiding something.

* * * * *

Drogan guided his horse toward the forest. He needed to talk to Cade again, if Cade let himself be seen.

"You're quiet," Grayson said from beside him.

"Just thinking. I don't like this. Any of this."

"None of us do."

Drogan scanned the trees. "It was good to talk to him, almost as if years hadn't passed since we had last shared a meal. Cade is a good man. He shouldn't have to suffer all this alone."

"He isn't, apparently. He has Francesca."

"And the curse? Did you forget that?" he asked and glanced at Grayson.

"I can't forget the curse. You and Serena broke it, and I believe Adrianna and I have as well."

"You don't think Cade and Francesca can?"

Grayson shrugged one shoulder. "It's not that. Cade believes he'll die in this battle, and there was something in Fran's eyes this morning. Something I can't quite put my finger on."

"I saw it, too. She's frightened, but not in the way we think. She has a secret."

"That she does. Did she share it with Cade?"

"Maybe we'll find out."

Grayson snorted. "Francesca isn't reckless. She won't endanger herself or anyone she cares about. Maybe it is her worry over Cade. If Cade is as protective as you say, he won't let her do anything that could put her in harm's way."

"Nay, he won't."

"I owe him a great debt," Grayson said after a moment of silence. "One I fear I might not ever be able to repay."

Drogan looked at Grayson. "There is much I owe Cade for. He's always been there for his friends. We were the ones who failed him when he needed us the most. I won't fail him again."

"Count me in on whatever you're planning."

"Agreed, though I'd rather our wives not know."

Grayson chuckled. "I agree completely."

* * * * *

Cade knelt beside a tree and studied the ground. He knew the moment Grayson and Drogan came into the forest. It would be easy to disappear, but it was past time he stopped hiding from Drogan. It didn't take long for the riders to find him. Cade had walked a stretch of the river when Grayson and Drogan came into view.

"I'm surprised you let me find you," Drogan said.

Cade shrugged as he stood. "I'd prefer you stay in the castle as I asked, but I realized you'd want to look over the land. There is flooding down the river."

"I assumed as much. Were any of the cottages damaged?"

"A few were burned from the lightning strikes. I counted twelve trees down as well. One fell on a home. It's good that you got everyone inside the castle walls when you did."

Grayson shifted atop his horse. "Did you find anything else?"

Cade glanced at the tall, black-haired knight. "I did. Someone has been in the forest."

He squatted beside the tree and pointed to the track he had found. Drogan and Grayson dismounted and squatted beside him.

"There," Cade said and traced his finger over the print. "It's only half a print, but it's a boot."

"And large," Grayson said. "Definitely a man."

"Possibly one of my people," Drogan said and leaned close to the ground.

Cade shook his head. "It's leading away from the castle, and it's fresh. This happened last night during the storm." He straightened. "Someone was watching the castle."

"Or you," Drogan said as he too stood.

Grayson sighed. "Have you checked the rest of the forest?"

"Only a part of it," Cade said. "This is close enough to the sea that many would think it would be a good way to gain entrance to the castle."

Drogan said, "They can't get in, even if they wanted to."

Cade glanced at his hands. "Have you seen to the men I killed yesterday?"

"I sent a group to burn the bodies, if anything is left. It would take too long to bury them, and I want everyone back inside the walls as soon as possible. Including you."

Cade found he wanted to smile. It felt good to have someone care about him.

Like Francesca?

"Nay," Cade said. "I won't come inside. I need to stay out here so I can fight."

Grayson took a step toward him. "You can't think to battle him alone. Nigel will come with an army."

"I know. I'll be ready for them."

"Then let us help," Grayson urged.

Cade looked from Grayson to Drogan and back again. "I wish I could, but I cannot. Nigel will use you against me."

"He's right," Drogan said. "Damn, but I hate this. You shouldn't have to battle him alone, Cade."

"I'm the only one strong enough. I've released the darkness once, I'll do it again. That alone will allow me to best him," Cade said. "I won't give up until he's dead. That I promise you."

"Then understand Fran intends to make sure you live," Grayson said.

Cade's heart leapt at the mention of his witch. He wanted to ask how she was, if she was angry at him for sending her away. He missed her so much already that it felt as if his heart had left with her.

"She doesn't understand," Cade finally said.

Drogan lifted a brow. "I think maybe she does. She doesn't plan to give up on you, and she has inspired our wives as well. They are together now, determining how they can combine their magic to ensure you live."

The kernel of hope Francesca had planted in his chest grew, and he cursed his weakness. He wanted a future, one that included his witch, but he knew the only way Nigel would ever be defeated was if he gave the man all of himself.

Once he did, it would all be over. No magic could change that.

Cade drew in a deep breath. "Grayson, your men who have set up camp outside the walls are in danger."

"They're already moving inside the castle walls," Grayson said. "I never thanked you for saving Adrianna."

"And you as well, I hear," Cade said.

Grayson shrugged. "I only hold enough magic to heal myself."

"Still, it is something special. I wonder if Nigel plans on trying to kill you with the other witches."

Drogan crossed his arms over his chest. "It's a possibility we've already considered. Nigel knows Grayson holds some magic."

Cade fingered the hilt of his dagger, his thoughts turning to Nigel and what the evil sack of wine planned.

"What are you thinking?" Drogan asked.

"The storms are over."

"Aye. What of it?" Grayson asked.

Cade glanced at the river, prickles of unease rushing over his skin. "Any lord who cares for his people would be riding his land, making sure everything was all right, and giving assistance to those who require it. Any lord who cared would put aside his safety to ensure his people."

"What are you getting at?" Drogan asked.

Cade jerked and palmed his knives. "Get to the castle. It's a trap!" he yelled as the first round of arrows whooshed around them.

Grayson tried to mount his horse, but an arrow lodged in his left shoulder. He cursed and fell off his horse. Cade rushed to his side and helped him astride the animal, dodging the arrows that continued to rain upon them.

"They're in the trees," Drogan murmured as he winced from an arrow in his leg. Another embedded itself in his horse's chest. The horse screamed and reared before he fell onto his side, trapping Drogan's leg beneath his weight.

"Go," Cade yelled at Grayson, but the knight refused.

Grayson jumped from his horse and slapped him on the withers so that it raced toward the castle. The next thing he knew, Grayson was beside him, helping him pull Drogan free. Cade bit back a groan when an arrow sunk into his back by his shoulder. He reached around and broke off the arrow.

"How many?" Drogan asked.

Grayson's lips pulled back as he tugged at Drogan. "Too damn many."

"I should have listened, Cade."

Cade ground his teeth together and ignored the stinging in his shoulder. When Drogan was finally free, he and Grayson put Drogan between them, his arms draped over their shoulders as they raced toward the sea dodging more arrows.

Drogan's face was devoid of color once they finally reached the secret entrance to the castle. Blood poured from all three of them.

"Get the damn arrow out before Serena sees it," Drogan said.

While Grayson held him steady, Cade pulled the arrow from Drogan's leg. Blood rushed from the wound.

"Me next," Grayson said.

Once Drogan was leaning against the rocks, Cade pulled the arrows from Grayson's front and one from the back of his arm.

"Done," Cade said. "Get inside. And stay inside."

"Wait," Drogan said. "What about your wound?"

Cade shrugged and immediately regretted it. "It's nothing. I'll be fine."

Grayson stepped toward him. "You can't get the arrow out yourself. Let me help."

Cade wished it was Francesca with him, soothing him with her soft hands and gentle touch. She had wanted to tend to his side and leg after the wolf, and now he wished he had let her. Those injuries weren't completely healed, and now this new wound would make fighting that much more difficult.

He nodded to Grayson and turned so he could reach the arrow. Cade placed his hands on the rocks near Drogan and took a deep breath. On his second breath, Grayson jerked the arrow free. Cade fell to his knees as a wave of dizziness assaulted him. Blood rushed from the wound, soaking his tunic. He rose on shaky legs and faced Drogan and Grayson.

"Prepare. Nigel is on his way."

"What of the men in the forest?" Grayson asked.

Drogan shook his head. "They'll be gone by the time we gather men to look for them. They did exactly what they were sent to do."

"Make us worry. And wonder," Cade said. "There is no telling when or where the next attack will take place."

Grayson helped Drogan stand, and they started toward the secret entrance.

"Are you sure you don't want to come?" Grayson asked. "Adrianna could heal you."

"The wound is nothing. Go see your wives."

Cade waited until they were gone before he let himself reach for the rocks to hold himself up. It took a great amount of effort to make it to the cave, and even then, he wasn't sure he could build a fire.

The blood wouldn't stop, and he had to clean the wound. It was just like Nigel to use some kind of poison or other evil to tip the arrows.

"Shite," Cade murmured and turned toward the sea.

The salt in the water would help to clean the wound, and if he was lucky, stop the bleeding. He stumbled and fell in the sand so that he had to crawl the rest of the way to the water. He was hidden from view from the forest by the rocks, but Cade didn't want to get too far from the cave, just in case.

He moved deep enough into the water so that he could sit down facing the castle and let the waves crash against him. He hissed in pain as the salt met his wounds. His gaze strayed to the castle, wondering what Francesca was doing and if she was thinking of him.

Fool.

"Aye, fool," the darkness mocked. *"Everything could have been ours!"*

Cade closed his eyes, refusing to acknowledge the darkness. But he knew from past experience that the darkness wouldn't be ignored.

Chapter Seventeen

Francesca stood in the doorway to Grayson and Adrianna's chamber, where Adrianna healed Drogan. Grayson was healing himself, and Serena was scolding both men for leaving the castle. The men had already finished their tale of how they had been in the forest talking to Cade when the attack came.

"What of Cade?" Francesca asked. Her heart beat so loud she feared it would leap from her chest. "Is he hurt?"

When Grayson and Drogan exchanged glances, anger blossomed within her. "You left him to see to his own wounds? You left him?"

Serena left her husband's side and walked to Francesca. "I'm sure they had good reason not to bring Cade inside."

"Aye," Grayson said. "He didn't want to come."

"He's wounded, isn't he?" Francesca asked.

Drogan nodded. "He took an arrow in the back of the shoulder."

Francesca turned on her heel without another word. She was going to get her herbs and see to Cade herself, regardless of whether he wanted to see her or not. The thought of him alone, injured and in pain, made her heart clench.

"Wait," Adrianna said. "I'll go with you, Fran."

"Nay," Grayson said at the same time Drogan yelled for Francesca to halt.

Grayson grabbed Drina's shoulders and turned her to face him. "I won't let you go out there and get hurt."

"But you'll allow a man who saved you, twice now, to sit in pain!" Francesca yelled.

She wasn't sure what was wrong with her. She never raised her voice, and when she was angry, no one knew it because she hid it so well. Yet when it came to Cade, her emotions were out of control.

Francesca turned to Drogan. "Don't you dare try to stop me from going to him."

This time when she walked away, there were no shouts for her to stop. She hurried to her chamber for her bag of herbs. It was too bad Adrianna couldn't come with her. She could heal Cade much faster than the herbs could.

But Francesca understood why Grayson had told her nay. He was only looking out for the one he loved.

* * * * *

"I've never seen her so...emotional," Serena said as she stared after Francesca's retreating back.

"It's Cade," Drogan said. "There is more there than either of them admits."

She turned to her husband. "You shouldn't have left him. He wouldn't have left you."

"I couldn't very well force him inside, love. We were more injured than he was, so we couldn't overpower him."

She sighed and glanced at Grayson and Drina. "You all could have been killed."

"In case you missed it," Grayson said drily, "we nearly were."

Adrianna took a deep breath. "I didn't say anything before, because I didn't want to upset Fran, but the arrows were dipped in some kind of poison."

"No wonder it's taking so long to heal," Grayson mumbled.

"The poison wasn't meant to kill, but it was meant to slow you down and cause great pain. I need to go with Fran. If Cade is injured, she's going to need my help. Besides, he did save us."

"I know," Grayson said.

Drogan stood. "We'll all go."

"You're not fully healed," Drina said. "Both of you should rest."

Grayson raised a brow. "If you're going, I'm going."

"Same for me," Drogan said as he looked to Serena.

Serena nodded. "Then let us go now. Fran shouldn't have to do this alone."

* * * * *

Francesca ran from the secret tunnel to Cade's cave only to find it in darkness.

"Cade," she called.

The sunlight only reached halfway into the cave, not even close to where the fire usually was. She used her hands to feel her way along the cave, calling out to Cade as she went. With each heartbeat, she feared she would find him dead. With each step, she cursed Drogan and Grayson for leaving him when he was wounded.

The relief she felt when Cade wasn't to be found in the cave was short lived. Where could he have gone? Had Nigel's men found him wounded and weak and taken him somewhere?

She rushed out of the cave to return to Drogan and ask for his help, but then she spotted something on the beach. Her lips parted on a cry as she realized it was Cade, lying in the waves on shore. His knives were discarded in the sand, and it appeared he had tried to remove his tunic.

Her feet stumbled as she ran to him. She knelt beside him, mindless of the waves that swarmed her or the sand. Her hand shook as she moved it to his chest to see if his heart still beat.

"Thank God," she murmured when she found him still alive.

Now came the hard part—moving him from the water to the cave. She stood, her sodden skirts weighing her down as she moved to Cade's head and tried to pick him up under his arms. She didn't budge him at all, but she did manage to see a part of his wound.

"That's in the sand," she murmured into the wind.

She tried to lift him again. She had to get him inside the cave so she could tend to the wound, but determination alone wasn't going to move Cade.

"Let us," Drogan said as he walked up beside her.

Francesca blinked, looking from Drogan to Grayson. She backed away only to find Adrianna and Serena on either side of her.

"What are you all doing here?" she asked.

Adrianna smiled. "Helping. Now, while the men are getting Cade, take me to the cave. We're going to need a fire."

Francesca watched as Drogan and Grayson hefted Cade to his feet so Drogan could carry him over his shoulder. Grayson cut away Cade's soaked tunic and tossed it aside before grabbing Cade's weapons.

"Fran," Serena urged.

She nodded and hurried to the cave. Francesca showed Serena where the wood was while she smoothed out the blankets for Cade to lie on. It wasn't long before the crackle of a fire filled the cave.

Francesca held her breath, watching Drogan kneel down on one knee and Grayson hold Cade by the shoulders as they lowered him to the blanket. Cade's face was pale, his breathing shallow.

She started to get the bag of herbs she'd dropped when she first came into the cave looking for Cade, but Adrianna was already kneeling beside him.

"Turn him on his side toward you," Drina instructed Grayson.

Francesca fisted her hands, her heart beating so hard it hurt. She got her first look at Cade's wound. The arrow had been pulled out cleanly, and the salt water had probably done it some good, but it was coated in sand.

She started forward to wipe away the sand when Drina lifted a wet rag from a bowl of water she hadn't seen Serena place beside her. Drogan removed Cade's boots, and Serena helped to hold Cade still. Francesca had never felt so helpless.

Once the sand was gone, Drina laid her hands over Cade's wound and closed her eyes. Not once had Francesca ever been jealous of another *bana-bhuidseach's* power. Until now. She was good with her herbs. Good enough to heal Cade herself.

Though she knew it was silly, she hated to have someone else mend him. She watched Drina with baited breath, her gaze never leaving Cade. It took longer than Drogan's healing had, but finally Cade's breathing returned to normal. Drina lowered her hands and opened her eyes to Grayson.

"Lower him onto his back gently," Drina instructed.

As soon as Grayson laid Cade back and stepped aside, Francesca moved to Cade. She sat beside him, hating how there was nothing for her to do.

"Thank you," she said. "All of you. I know how dangerous it was for you to leave the castle."

Drina smiled as Grayson helped her to stand. "It might be awhile before he wakes. There was poison on the arrows. They didn't use much, just enough to cause pain and make the wounds difficult to heal."

"Everything will be alright now," Serena said.

Francesca nodded and turned her gaze to Drogan and Grayson, who stood closer to the entrance.

"We'll stay until he wakes," Drogan said.

Grayson grunted. "I say we move him into the castle."

Drogan shook his head. "Cade would never forgive me. I respect why he doesn't want to come inside, and I won't force him, even if it is for his own good."

Francesca waited until Serena and Adrianna walked to their husbands before she intertwined her fingers with Cade's. Her gaze stayed on his chest, watching it rise and fall regularly. She hadn't liked the stark fear she had felt when she saw him on the beach. Until she'd felt for herself, she was sure he'd been dead. And the vengeance that coursed through her had been violent, frightening so.

Now that he had been healed and was sleeping, Francesca found it impossible to keep her eyes open. But she didn't want to sleep and miss Cade waking. She also wished the others would leave so she could be alone with Cade.

He would be furious that she wasn't in the castle, but she didn't care. His life meant more than hers. Besides, it wasn't her time to die.

Francesca leaned her head against the cave wall and let her eyes shut. At the entrance, she could hear the others talking amongst themselves. She wondered what they were saying, but she couldn't make out the words.

Then she didn't care as sleep claimed her.

* * * * *

Cade came awake and realized he was no longer in the sea. Had he crawled to the cave? As he checked his body for the injury, he didn't feel anything. Other than a warm hand holding his. He cracked open his eyes to find Francesca beside him, leaning against the wall, asleep.

"How do you feel?"

Cade jerked his head to the other side to find Drogan squatting across the fire. "Like hell," he answered. "What are you doing here?"

"We came to help."

At the "we," Cade looked around the cave and saw Serena, Adrianna and Grayson. "None of you should be here."

"The arrow was dipped in poison," Adrianna said. "I realized it as I was healing Drogan."

Serena placed her hands on Drogan's shoulders. "When Fran grasped you were also injured, she came to help."

Cade inhaled deeply. "Foolish woman. She's going to get herself killed."

"Tell her that," Grayson murmured.

Cade started to sit up when Adrianna's hand on his shoulder stopped him.

"Rest some more," she urged.

He nodded and stared into the fire, his thumb rubbing circles on the back of Francesca's hand. "Thank you," he told them.

"With all you've done for us, it's the least we could do," Serena said.

Cade tried not to look at Francesca, but he couldn't help himself. "You should return to the castle. Take the witch with you, too. It's too risky for her to be out here."

Drogan shook his head. "I want to make sure you're completely healed before I leave. Until then, you're stuck with us."

Cade noticed Adrianna was watching Francesca, her brow puckered in concern. "What is it?" he asked.

"I'm surprised Fran hasn't woken while we've been talking."

Drogan stood. "She's been through a lot over the past couple of days. None of us have slept well. Maybe she feels safe enough to rest now."

Cade hoped they were right. The thought of someone harming his witch made him want to kill something.

"Yes," the darkness hissed.

Cade clenched his jaw. He fought against the rising tide of the darkness, concentrating on Francesca until he was once more in control. He wasn't used to having so many people around, and it made him nervous and antsy to be up and around. Anything to get them to leave him and his witch alone.

"I know that look," Drogan said.

"What look?"

"The look that says you want us gone."

Cade shrugged. "I'm used to my privacy."

"You're too damned used to being alone."

Cade didn't argue. It was the truth. He spent so much time alone, protecting everyone from himself, that he didn't know what to do around people anymore.

Except his witch.

It was different with Francesca. Everything was different with her.

Cade glanced at Drogan to find his gold eyes watching him.

"I'm sorry," Drogan suddenly said.

Cade frowned. "For what?"

"For not doing something that day."

Cade didn't need to know which day Drogan referred to. It was the day the darkness had claimed Cade. He could hate Drogan for it, but the blame was solely on one person's shoulders—his own.

"Nay," Cade said. "You've nothing to apologize for."

Drogan ran a hand down his face and sighed as he sat across the fire. "I shoul've done something."

"There was nothing you or anyone could have done. Nigel wanted me, and he stopped at nothing to get me."

Drogan's gaze caught his. "What did Nigel threaten you with? It wasn't us, was it?"

"Nay," he murmured. Cade almost refused to tell him, but then realized there was no use now. "He used my family against me. My youngest sister, Amelia, had caught his attention. He threatened to make her his and kill the rest if I didn't do what he wanted."

"God's blood," Drogan cursed. "Why didn't you tell us? We could have gone to the king or got them out of the castle until we could kill Nigel. He hadn't acquired the power he does now. He would have been easy to kill."

Cade sighed. He had been over that day in his head a million times, wondering how things would have turned out if he had done something—anything—differently. In the end, he realized there was no use wondering how things could have been.

"I knew if I brought you and Gerard into it, Nigel would turn to your families as well. I couldn't live with myself if something had happened."

Drogan swallowed. "I learned a few years ago that your family...."

"Died," Cade finished for him.

"Maybe that's a blessing, since Nigel couldn't use them against you anymore."

Cade was more relieved that Drogan didn't ask how they died. It was one of the many shames he would carry with him into Hell.

"That's when you left Nigel, isn't it?" Drogan asked.

Cade nodded. "I knew if I stayed longer, Nigel would come up with something else to blackmail me with. I couldn't allow that to happen."

"We'll get through this, Cade. You'll see."

Cade didn't argue with Drogan as he rose and walked back to the others at the entrance. He pushed thoughts of Nigel from his mind and thought of the many—and various—ways he wanted to make love to his witch.

He grinned, turning his head to look at her. Aye, as soon as they were alone, he was going to strip her out of the cream gown and kiss every inch of her skin.

After all, it might be the last time they were together before Nigel arrived.

Chapter Eighteen

Francesca sucked in a breath as she stared at the forest. She knew this was a dream vision by the slowness in which everything moved.

She stood atop the battlements, the wind whipping around her. Because this vision didn't involve her, not only could she not feel the wind, but she couldn't move either. Whatever she was supposed to see was in the forest.

Her stomach fell to her feet when she spotted Cade. She tried desperately to move, to run from the castle and into the woods to see what was happening to him. He moved swiftly through the forest, as though he had seen his quarry and was hunting it.

Francesca focused all her power on Cade, and in a blink, she was in the forest. Cade had paused beside a cluster of trees. His knives were in his hands, and he was getting ready to attack a group of men.

Cade never saw the hole in the ground. His foot slipped inside it as he jumped. There was a loud pop as Cade's leg broke. He grabbed it, pain lacing his features.

And then Nigel was standing over him, an evil smile on his hawkish face.

The dream faded, only to be replaced with her standing in front of Nigel, as she had dreamed for so many years. The wind whipped at her skirts, wrapping the material around her legs.

Nigel laughed and beckoned her to try her magic on him. Since this dream involved her, Francesca could move around at will. And she felt everything twice as intensely as she did while awake.

She lifted her hands to block the evil Nigel threw at her. Until recently, she had always been able to deflect it and gather her magic to kill him. But not anymore. Now, the evil enveloped her, smothering her in the inky blackness. She screamed and tried to move, but the darkness held her firm as the evil began to claw at her skin.

Francesca's eyes flew open. Her chest hurt as if she'd run miles. Strong fingers curled around her hand, and she looked down to find Cade watching her. Had she called out or given any hint of the vision she was having?

"That makes twice now I've seen you wake in such a fashion. Are they nightmares?" he asked, concern crinkling his brow.

She tried to smile, but the fear in her veins would loosen its hold. "Of a sort. A vision."

"Not a good one, I gather."

Francesca shook her head and remembered the sound of Cade's leg breaking. As awful as that was, it was better than the evil attacking her. She couldn't understand why before, she had always seen herself beating Nigel, but now she saw him besting her. Had his power grown so much? Or had hers weakened?

"Can you tell me?"

She swallowed, wishing with all her might that she could share what she'd seen. But she had always kept to herself her visions that involved Nigel.

"My visions are snatches of a dream. It's difficult to piece together," she lied, praying he would forgive her.

For a moment, Cade stared at her. "If you don't want to tell me, that's fine. There's no need to lie."

Tears pricked the back of her eyes. "I want to tell. I wish I could."

"I know the feeling well," he said after a moment's hesitation. "Can you tell the others?"

She shook her head.

"It isn't good for you to carry such a weight alone, witch. You should share it with someone. How often do you have this...vision?"

"Every night."

He lifted his brows. "Will it ever go away?"

"When what I see is carried through, then, aye, it will cease to plague me."

His thumb caressed the back of her hand, lending her strength. "Do you know when that will be?"

She could see by the set of his jaw he had an idea it had to do with Nigel. In no way could he discover what she had to do. She knew without a doubt he would stop her.

"Nay," she said, and it wasn't a complete lie.

Thankfully, he didn't ask any more questions. Francesca glanced to the front of the cave to find the others. She was surprised they had stayed.

"I wish they would leave," Cade murmured. "You as well. It's dangerous here."

"It is dangerous everywhere."

He grunted. Her gaze strayed to his chest and abdomen to the waist of his breeches. Aye, she wished the others would leave as well.

"Cease, witch," he ground out. "My blood heats with you near, and if you continue to stare at me like that, I'll take you right here."

She should have been shocked at his words, but instead, a thrill rushed through her. She looked into his blue eyes and saw the desire there. She smiled as desire heated her own blood.

"Witch," he warned.

"I can't help it."

He rose and walked to the back of the cave until the shadows took him. Francesca felt his absence immediately. She'd known him only a few days, but it was if her body had known him for eternity.

And my heart.

Her heart? She bit back a groan. Her feelings for him were strong, and she feared they were turning into love. Francesca used the rocks behind her to help her to her feet. She glanced at the shadows where Cade had moved before she walked to the others.

"Did you rest well?" Adrianna asked as she joined them.

Francesca nodded, but the way Drogan watched her told her he knew she'd had a vision. She could hide most anything from anyone except Cade and Drogan. Drogan had known her since she was a child, so it was only natural that he would sense her emotions.

But what about Cade?

"Cade wants us back in the castle," Grayson said. "The more I look at the beach, the more I realize how easy it would be for Nigel to attack here."

"He won't," Cade said as he strode up with a new tunic on and his weapons back in place. "The other side of the castle is braced by razor-sharp rocks. No army could slip through that without being seen. The only way to the back of the castle is on this side, and I won't let them through."

Drogan, his arms crossed over his chest, stared at the sea. "How many of Nigel's men tried to attack Grayson and Drina?"

Grayson shrugged and looked at Cade.

Cade absently scratched his shoulder. "About three score."

"Sixty?" Drina repeated.

Drogan faced Cade. "How many do you think Nigel will bring with him?"

"Hundreds."

Drogan cursed, and Serena wrapped her hands around his arm.

Francesca listened to all of it with interest. She'd seen Nigel's army in her vision.

"Francesca," Drogan said. "Have you had any visions on this? Anything that would help?"

She kept her gaze from moving to Cade, but she felt his on her anyway. Her eyes locked with Drogan's. She hated lying to him, but there was no other way. Still, maybe she could give some information.

"Aye."

Grayson took a step toward her, his face mottled with anger. "When were you going to tell us?"

Cade stepped between them, his hand on his dagger. "Don't talk to her that way."

She wanted to wrap her arms around him and bury her head in his neck, to feel Cade's warmth and strength surround her. No man had ever taken up for her like that before, and she found she loved it.

"Grayson has a right to be angry," Drogan said.

"He can take his anger out on me then."

Francesca touched Cade's shoulder. He turned his head to look at her, and she grinned. "Thank you, but they do have a right to be angry. I should've told them."

Cade turned toward her and moved his head to her ear. "Is this what you dreamed about? What has frightened you so?"

She nodded, wondering why she answered him when she knew he would want to know more. He sighed and straightened only to move beside her.

Francesca licked her lips. "Nigel will bring hundreds and hundreds of men. They will surround the castle from one side to the other. The only place they won't be is in the water."

"Why, I wonder?" Serena said. "You would think Nigel would attack everywhere."

"He's leaving us a way out," Drogan commented. "He wants us to get in the water so he can kill us then."

Adrianna shuddered. "With another storm?"

"Most likely," Drogan said.

Francesca wished she could alleviate their fears, but if they were thinking of a way to protect themselves, they wouldn't be worrying over her. Which would give her the time she needed to sneak out of the castle and confront Nigel.

"Witch," Cade whispered next to her, "promise me you'll be in the castle with the others."

She looked at him, wondering again why such a handsome man would want her, but thankful just the same. "Where else would I be?"

"I don't know, but you have a look about you that says you're hiding something. You're leaving something out."

She glanced at the others to find them still talking about Nigel's men. She leaned into Cade and inhaled his scent of orangewood, salt and man. "You smell good."

He snorted. "I'm covered in salt and dried blood."

"You always smell good to me."

"Stop changing the subject. What do you have planned?"

She shook her head. "Don't make me lie to you. Please. I'm not putting anyone in danger."

"And yourself?"

"I could ask you the same thing."

"You can ask me that, knowing what I am?"

"I can ask you that, knowing what you are."

For a moment, she thought he would kiss her. His eyes blazed with emotion before he lowered his gaze to her mouth and leaned towards her. Their lips were breaths apart, her heart skidding in her chest when Drogan called her name.

Cade sighed and straightened. Francesca had no choice but to face Drogan.

"Have you seen where Nigel will be?" Drogan asked, his gaze intense and his brow furrowed in concentration.

Grayson nodded. "Aye. If we could locate him and kill him, his army would scatter."

Francesca swallowed and shook her head. "Nigel is everywhere. And nowhere."

"I've already told you, he's mine," Cade all but growled beside her as he took a step toward Drogan.

Drogan held up a hand. "Easy, Cade. I don't much care how the bastard dies as long as he dies. You want to do it, I understand, but if we get a clear shot, we'll take it."

"Nay," Francesca said. She had hoped Serena or Adrianna would stop the talk, but neither seemed inclined to do anything other than listen. "Nay."

"I already said I would stay within the walls, Fran," Drogan bit out. "You want me to hide like the women and children?"

Serena bristled at his tone. "Women and children? Is that all we are to you?"

Grayson sighed. "We've already been through this the first time Nigel attacked. War is for men. Women have no place in it."

"Really?" Adrianna bit out, her gaze hard as she stared at her husband. "I beg to differ. Women are as involved, if not more, than the men. Who is it that heals the wounded? Who is it that readies the dead for burial? Who is it that cooks and cleans for the warriors who survived? Who is it that opens her arms at night for the warrior to take some refuge? Women. So don't you dare tell me war isn't for women. Its men who make the war, and we're left to clean everything up."

Francesca bit back a smile at the anger flashing in Drina's blue eyes. She was a perfect match for Grayson in every way.

Serena nodded. "Well said, Drina."

"Everyone must stay out of Nigel's sight," Cade said. "He'll use you all against me and each other. Don't give him the leverage."

"I brought a hundred and fifty men," Grayson said. "Combined with Drogan's three hundred, we can fight Nigel."

Cade snorted. "And you'll be massacred."

"He can't have control of all of them," Drogan said. "Does he?"

Cade shrugged. "I don't know for sure. Liam wasn't under Nigel's control, but who's to say about the others?"

"What about the men you killed who were going to attack us?" Adrianna asked.

"They had no power, if that's what you're asking."

Drogan nodded. "Then it stands to reason that we can beat Nigel."

Francesca became frantic. If Drogan and Grayson left the castle with their men, her battle with Nigel might never take place. And she wouldn't be able to kill him.

"What if Cade's right?" she asked. "What if Nigel has given these...men...some kind of power? They will cut through you easily. Then who is left to defend the castle?"

Drogan ran a hand down his face. "I'm a warrior, Fran. This is what I do."

"You're also a husband and father," Serena said.

Francesca knew Drogan was thinking over all that had been said. He wanted to fight, as did Grayson, but she knew she had to get to Nigel before they left the castle. She knew Drogan well enough to know that he wouldn't stay behind his walls long. The need for vengeance, for death, was strong in all the men.

Her gaze moved to Cade to find him watching her. The vivid blue of his eyes held her immobile, her heart accelerating. If only she hadn't taken so long to find Cade. If only she'd had all these past months to spend with him, learning about him, loving him.

She tore her gaze from him and walked out of the cave to the water's edge. She hadn't wanted to fall in love with Cade, but from the fist moment she had looked into his eyes, she'd been lost.

With her arms wrapped around her and the wind lifting the hair from her face, Francesca looked out over the seat to Phineas' castle.

It had been days since she'd seen the man who had been father and protector. To her shame, she hadn't thought much about him, not since that first meeting with Cade. She needed to check on Phineas, but with the threat of Nigel approaching any day, she couldn't take the chance.

She was a coward. She should tell the others what her vision was, let them know she was the key to defeating Nigel despite Cade's protests. She was the one who had been having the visions since she was ten. She was the one with the power.

She was the *bana-bhuidseach*.

But she knew Drogan, Grayson, and even Cade well enough to know they would never allow her outside the gates. Even Serena and Adrianna were likely to stop her.

Despite being surrounded by so many people she considered friends, she was still alone. In another life, another future, there might have been a chance for her and Cade. There might have been love and happiness between them. Yet it was all wishful thinking, for she was in the present, and the present was filled with an evil who wanted them all dead.

Chapter Nineteen

Cade stayed in the cave despite his body's urging him to follow Francesca. Her eyes had held such sorrow, such resolve, that he knew she withheld information from them about Nigel.

Grayson, Adrianna and Serena slowly walked from the cave, leaving only him and Drogan. Cade waited for Drogan to talk, for it was obvious his old friend had already formed a plan.

"What's your plan?" Drogan asked. "Will you lie in wait for Nigel?"

"Nay. I plan to draw him out."

Drogan scratched his jaw. "How are you going to do that?"

"He wants me. He's coming for me. He'll be looking."

"I want to help."

Cade sighed. "I wish you could, but I've seen him fight enough to know exactly what he'll do. I'm asking you, as a friend, as a brother, not to let that happen."

"You leave me little choice."

"Give me time to fight Nigel."

Drogan's lips thinned. "And if you lose?"

"Then you and your men can attack."

After a moment, Drogan nodded. "I give you my word I will allow you time to attack Nigel—but be warned, Cade, I refuse to allow you to die."

Cade watched his friend stride from the cave to the others who stood waiting for him. He didn't deserve a friend like Drogan.

Or the witch.

His gaze instantly found Francesca, her red hair like flames against the cream of her gown and the dark blue of the water. The more he was around her, the harder it became to let her go. So much so that he realized he had to make her understand she could never return to him.

Cade walked to his witch. As soon as he reached her, she turned to face him. He wanted to take her in his arms, to promise her that everything would be all right. But Cade never gave a promise he couldn't keep, and he wasn't sure what this venture's outcome would be.

"Every hour draws Nigel closer," he said.

"I know. I wish I could have a vision of when he would arrive."

"It wouldn't matter. We are as prepared as we can be. Will you give me your vow that you will stay in the castle, safe?"

She smiled and placed her right hand over his heart. "I vow that I will stay as safe as anyone can when Nigel arrives."

"He'll be looking for you." Cade wrapped his hand around hers at his chest. "I wish I could be beside you to keep you safe."

Her lips curved into a slow, sensual smile. "Don't you realize you're always with me?"

His balls tightened as his gaze moved to her lips. He wanted another kiss, one more that would last him from then until his death. One more taste of paradise, regardless of who watched.

Cade cupped the back of her head and brought his head down to hers. He covered her mouth and held still for a moment before he slid his tongue past her lips. She moaned and grabbed his shoulder with her free hand.

He took her mouth again and again, giving her all the desire, the hope, the hunger he held inside for her. His cock throbbed with need when he finally broke the kiss.

"Cade," she whispered.

"You cannot return here," he said and brought his face to hers. "No matter what you hear, what you see, or even what you dream. You cannot return. Give me your vow."

She blinked and licked her kiss-swollen lips. "You ask too much."

"I ask for your safety. It would kill me if anything happened to you. Please, witch. Give me your word."

She reluctantly nodded her head. "I could help you, like before, when the darkness claims you."

"There won't be a need again."

Cade had known forcing her away would be difficult. He just hadn't expected it to hurt so damn bad.

"How do you feel?" she asked.

"Better. All my wounds are healed."

She glanced away. "You should have let me use my herbs after the wolf attack."

"Adrianna might have healed my body, but you healed my soul, witch. Never forget that."

Unable to help himself, he wrapped his arms around her and brought her against him. It felt so right to have her close to him, to feel her warmth, her goodness and her magic. He was going to miss her, and for a moment he considered going with them into the castle to hide away from Nigel.

But Cade knew it was useless. Nigel would never give up. Regardless of the hope that grew in his heart, Cade had but one option, and it didn't involve his witch.

He pushed her away from him. "Go. Go now," he said and gave her a small shove toward Drogan.

Francesca's tawny eyes held his for a moment. She didn't fight him, didn't cling. She straightened her shoulders and said, "Remember, Cade, you are a good man. I'll always be here if you need me. You have but to call, and I will come."

He couldn't watch her walk away. Already it felt as if someone had yanked out his heart, his chest hurt so badly. He faced the sea. He'd done the right thing sending her away—he was sure of it.

Then why does it feel so wrong?

He tensed when he felt someone move beside him. A glance confirmed it was Drogan.

"If things were different, I would demand you marry her," his friend said.

"If things were different, she'd already be mine."

Drogan sighed. "How is all this going to end, Cade? My family and my people are counting on me. They have no idea of the evil that stalks ever nearer."

Cade had no words to comfort him, not when he could find words to comfort himself. "I have one favor to ask of you."

"Name it," Drogan said and faced him.

He turned his head to Drogan. "Keep her safe. No matter what, don't let Nigel get her."

Drogan nodded. "I vow to you Fran will be safely hidden away with Serena and Adrianna."

"Thank you."

They clasped forearms before Drogan pulled him to his chest and slapped him on the back. Cade closed his eyes as he embraced his friend. It was likely to be the last time he saw any of them.

When he stepped back, Cade found Francesca standing by the entrance to the secret tunnel to the castle. The others had already gone through, but she stood solemnly, watching him. It took every ounce of effort for him to turn away from her instead of running to her, pulling her into his arms and to a future together.

Cade didn't slow until he was back in his cave, but everywhere he looked, he saw Francesca. He smelled lilacs and felt magic in every stone of the cave. He slumped before the fire and put his head in his hands. What had happened to him? How had one witch found her way into his heart so quickly?

But he knew the answer.

She'd been what his soul needed. She had touched him as no other ever had, and she'd accepted him for who he was. She had given him her body, her maidenhead.

Cade knew in his heart, if he were ever to have a future with any sort of happiness, it would be with Francesca. Without a doubt, he knew, his life would be complete as long as she was by his side.

The darkness laughed inside him, the sound evil and haunting. *"Nay, warrior. You are mine. The only future you have is with me!"*

It frightened Cade how easily he got used to the quiet of the darkness when Francesca was with him. The darkness had never feared anyone or anything until her. The fact that the witch could keep the evil not only quiet, but locked deep inside him, made his hunger for her grow.

Peace wasn't something he had felt since before he had joined the king's Royal Guards. Now that he had felt it again, he wasn't ready to let it go. He closed his eyes and pictured Francesca at the water, her fiery locks licking at him while her tawny gaze scorched him with the breath of her desire.

"Only a fool would have let the witch go," the darkness said. *"There's no escaping me now."*

Cade didn't want to escape it. He would need the darkness when he fought Nigel. He didn't fight against the darkness, but he didn't let the evil gain any control, either. Soon it would be time to give in. Until then, he had his memories of his witch to sustain him.

My witch.

* * * * *

141

It had been two days since Francesca had last seen Cade. There wasn't a moment in the day—or night—that she didn't think about him, dream about him. He was everywhere, in everything she did.

Drogan and the others had kept a constant watch on her since their return from Cade. She had bided her time, deceiving them into believing she would indeed stay in the castle. They were her friends, and she hated to mislead them, but she had no choice. Cade's life was at stake.

Ever since she'd had the vision of him breaking his leg, she knew she had to get to the forest and find the hole before Nigel arrived. That hole would be the death of Cade, and that she couldn't live with.

He would survive Nigel's attack to live a long healthy life. Though he might not believe it, he was strong enough to beat the darkness within him. When he did, he would find a bright future awaiting him.

And a wife and children.

She ignored the lump of jealousy that thought brought. There was no reason for her to be envious, since she would be dead. Cade didn't know of her love, and she had no hold over him.

She stared into the empty hearth as she listened with half an ear to Grayson and Drogan discussing strategies for their attack. Serena and Drina were never far from their husbands. Even occupants of the castle had grown quieter with each passing day. Everyone knew an attack was coming, but they didn't know from whom.

Fear had enveloped the land. Where once children played and laughed in the bailey, it was now taken over by the knights readying for battle. The children watched, wild-eyed and silent, while mothers forced smiles and lied about everything being all right. Nothing was all right, and Francesca feared it might never be.

Her vision of Nigel had continued with the darkness taking her. Before, she'd had the knowledge she would defeat Nigel.

Now, she wasn't sure of anything. Her confidence had turned to fear.

She glanced at the couples around her. Serena held her son on her lap, making faces at the infant. He cooed and laughed in response. Adrianna looked longingly at the bairn. Francesca didn't think it would be long before she and Grayson welcomed a child.

The way both men looked hungrily at their wives made her think of Cade. As protective as he was, he would make an excellent husband and lord. He should have returned to his lands and taken control of his castle instead of running from Nigel.

She realized Drogan and Grayson had stopped talking. When she turned her gaze to Drogan, his face was a mask, with no emotion to be seen as he returned her stare.

"Walk with me," he said.

Francesca glanced at Serena, who shrugged, as Francesca rose.

They left the great hall and walked to the tower at the back of the castle that gave a clear view of the sea and Phineas' castle. Drogan had been silent, and Francesca knew he had something to say. He often came to the tower when he needed to think. It had been a favorite place of his as a child when he wanted to escape his cruel father.

Once in the tower, Francesca leaned against the wall, her hands behind her back as she waited. Drogan stood with his hands braced on the stones at the edge of the window.

"I've news from Phineas," Drogan finally said. His voice was so soft she almost didn't hear it.

She pushed away from the wall. "He's ill, isn't he? I knew I should've returned."

"He's not ill."

"Then what is it?"

Drogan faced her and pulled a parchment from his jerkin. "This came at dawn. There's one for you and one for me, from Phineas."

Dread began to creep its fingers around her. She tried to breath, but her lungs wouldn't work.

"He died just after midnight last night," Drogan said. "I was told his passing was peaceful."

"He was alone."

Francesca had always promised she would be by his side. Phineas had smiled and patted her hand and told her not to worry about an old man so.

Drogan took a deep breath. "He wanted to leave the castle to you, since he considered you his daughter. Since I'm his only surviving family, the castle has come to me, but it's yours to live in."

She reached behind her for the wall, anything to keep her steady on her feet. Phineas had been the one constant in her life, the one person she had always been able to count on.

"Do you want me to read his message to you?"

Francesca shook her head and reached for the letter. Phineas has taught her reading and writing as well as arithmetic. He had doted on her, loved her and sheltered her.

The tower blurred as tears fell down her cheeks. It wasn't until she wiped them away that she realized Drogan had left her. She held the rolled parchment in front of her. After a moment, she broke the seal and unrolled the missive.

My dearest Francesca,

As I lay here, the breath from my body bringing me closer and closer to death, I'm thankful for the time I had with you. Though you weren't my own, I considered you my daughter.

I would leave you my isle if I could, but it must pass to Drogan. He's already assured me that you will be allowed to live here for as long as you want. I never want you to think you do not have a home. You made my last years some of the happiest a man could wish for. I wish that same happiness for you.

Your mother once told me you had a great destiny ahead of you. I fear that destiny is Nigel. Though your mother never told me what it was you would do, she said it was important.

Godspeed, my daughter. God keep you safe.

May joy and love find their way to you.

P.

Francesca read the letter twice more. Her mother had known of her battle with Nigel, had known and never said anything? She wished she could have been able to talk to her mother about it, but by the time her visions began, her mother was already dead.

She stared at the distant castle through the window. "Godspeed, Phineas. Thank you for everything."

Francesca rolled the missive up and hurried to her chamber. Drogan would assume she was grieving in the tower, which would give her the time she needed to sneak out of the castle and find the hole in the forest.

With the parchment tucked away in her trunk, Francesca looked down at her dark green gown. It would blend well in the trees. She knew the secret exit near the sea was being watched by Drogan and Grayson. The only other way out was through the postern door in the castle walls.

She blew out a breath and walked from her chamber. She used the back stairs so she wouldn't run into Drogan and exited through the kitchen. Once in the bailey, it was easy for her to stay hidden with all the knights. Francesca wanted to hurry, but if she did, she would bring notice to herself, and she couldn't allow that.

She made a turn around the bailey, careful to keep her head down. When she reached the postern door the second time, she stopped and glanced around to see if anyone was watching. Then she reached to unlock the door when a voice stopped her.

"What are you doing?"

Chapter Twenty

Francesca sighed and turned to face Adrianna. Grayson's wife stood staring at her, one blonde brow raised in question.

"Are you trying to get yourself killed?" Adrianna asked. "Drogan wants us to stay in the castle."

"I know what Drogan wants."

Drina's eyes narrowed, and she took a step closer to Francesca. "Did you have a vision?"

The need to tell someone of her vision was too great to ignore. She nodded and pulled Drina close. "I have seen the outcome of this war. We will defeat Nigel."

"That's wonderful news. Why haven't you told anyone before now?"

"Because if there's one change, however small, it could adjust the outcome. I want nothing more than to assure Drogan his family and castle will survive, but I cannot. Nothing can change."

Drina nodded slowly. "Which is why you didn't tell us the size of Nigel's army or where he was attacking. Grayson is still upset about that."

"As he should be. I wish I could divulge everything I knew, but it is my wish to see everyone survive."

"I understand. Is that why you're sneaking out?"

Francesca glanced at the door. "Aye. I saw Cade get injured and Nigel's men kill him. I need to make sure that doesn't happen."

"You're risking your life."

"He's risking his for us."

Drina let out a breath and smiled. "Then I'm coming with you."

"What?"

"I love Grayson with all my heart, but the man needs to understand war involves women just as much as men."

Francesca chuckled. "Thank you, but, nay. I'll be fine."

"I'm coming, Fran."

She was wasting time arguing with Adrianna. "Make sure we're not followed," she murmured as she opened the door.

Francesca slipped out of the bailey, and Adrianna followed close behind her. With a glance in either direction, they rushed the short distance to the trees.

"Wait here and watch the door," Francesca said. "It's our only way back in."

Adrianna grabbed her hand as she was about to leave. "Be careful. I don't want to be the one to tell Cade something happened to you."

She knew Cade cared for her, or more importantly, that she was somehow able to help control the darkness within him. But did he care enough if she was to die?

"Cade...has enough to worry about."

"Don't fool yourself," Drina said. "I've seen the way he looks at you. There's desire there, but there's also something deeper. Love, perhaps?"

Francesca pulled her hand out of Adrianna's grasp. "You may have been able to beat the curse, but I won't."

"You've seen it?"

Francesca remained silent.

"And still you give yourself to Cade?"

"I give myself to Cade because I cannot deny what my heart wants. There is no future for us. We both know this."

Adrianna's eyes held a wealth of sadness. "Don't give up hope."

Francesca gave a quick nod and set out in the direction of the tree in her vision. She didn't know exactly where it was, but she knew she would be able to find it if given time. Time. Something she didn't have a lot of.

With her skirts in her hand, she hurried through the trees, searching for the gnarled oak, its thick trunk large enough to hide two grown men.

"There you are," she murmured when she caught sight of the tree.

Francesca ran to the tree and searched around the base until she found the hole. She knelt beside it to examine it more. The hole was two hands length deep and a span in diameter. Just enough for a man's foot to slip in and break his ankle or leg.

She rose and looked around for something to put in the hole. Then she spotted a large limb that had fallen during the recent storms. She gripped it and dragged it over to the oak, effectively covering the hole so that Cade would have to walk around it or jump over the limb. Either way, he wouldn't step in it.

Francesca dusted off her hands, a smile on her face, when something flew by her face to embed in the tree. She turned and saw an axe inches from her face. Someone grabbed her from behind and pinned her against the tree.

"God's blood, witch. Are you trying to get yourself killed?" Cade said through clenched teeth.

Francesca opened her mouth to talk when he silenced her with a look that told her he didn't want her to answer. Not now anyway.

"Stay here," he whispered.

She managed a nod before he moved away from her. Her heart hammered in her chest, and her veins turned to ice. She twisted her head to see Cade standing across from her, his feet braced apart and his knives in each hand.

"Someone looking for a fight?" he taunted.

Two men came at him at once, their swords long and broad. Cade easily leaned away from one and ducked underneath the other. As the two men passed him, he reached back with his knives and sunk them into the men's backs.

They slumped to the ground forgotten as Cade faced his next attackers. Francesca turned toward the tree and grasped the bark. It bit into her hands as she clung desperately to it, watching Cade wield his weapons with deadly skill.

He never missed, and he moved with the agility of a cat, the brawn of a wolf, and the annihilation of a dragon. But it was his face, a mask of determination and death, that set him apart from the others. He had no fear, no misgivings over what he was doing. He used his skill with his blades to cut down each and every man.

When he was the last one standing, she counted twelve corpses. Her gaze rose to him to find his eyes once more black as pitch. He threw his knives into the ground and stalked toward her. Blood splattered his clothes and hands as he spun her around until her back was pressed against the tree once more.

The darkness had taken him again, but she didn't fear him. Deep down, she knew the man inside fought against the evil, an evil he had let loose to protect her. She reached up and wiped a spot of blood from his cheek. His mouth covered hers, hard, demanding as he kissed her. Yet it didn't repulse her—it set her blood aflame.

Her arms wound around his neck, holding him close as he yanked up her skirts before lifting her so that her legs wrapped around his waist. Her body burned for his touch, to feel his rod thrusting hard and deep.

Cool air met the heated folds of her sex a heartbeat before Cade rubbed the head of his cock against her. She moaned and ground her hips against him. He guided his arousal to her entrance, and in one thrust, buried himself.

He groaned into her neck, clutching her hips. He held still for one heartbeat, two, before he began to plunge hard and fast. Francesca could do nothing but hold onto his shoulders as he brought her body to a heated frenzy of need.

Again and again he slammed into her, touching her womb and grinding against her pearl until she was mindless with desire.

Cade couldn't get enough of his witch. He wanted to mark her, brand her as his so no other man would dream of taking her away.

Each time he sunk into her, he could feel the darkness move and give away its hold on him. When her hands plunged into his hair and she whispered his name a moment before she stiffened in his arms, Cade gave into the need to mark her and bit her neck as his seed burst from him.

Her back arched, and she gasped, her arms tightening for a moment. Finally, Cade lifted his head and braced his forehead against hers. Shame washed over him for what he'd done.

"Don't you dare apologize," she said.

"I was a beast."

A smile pulled at her lips. "You were wonderful."

"I hurt you."

"Nay."

He wanted to believe her, to believe that she desired him as much as he desired her.

"I can still feel you inside me," she whispered.

The passion in her voice stirred his cock. He could have gotten them killed by taking her in the woods. He wouldn't be that careless again.

Cade pulled out of her and released her legs. While she straightened her skirts, he fastened his breeches. "Now tell me what you were doing out here. Alone."

"I'm not alone."

"Really? Who's with you?"

"Drina."

Cade cursed. Two witches. Alone in the forest. Grayson was going to have his head. "Where is Adrianna?"

"Near the castle, watching the postern door."

"Tell me why you came out here? What could be so important that you would risk your life?"

"You."

That pulled him up short. He searched her tawny eyes and saw the truth of it. "Me?"

"I had a vision of you stepping into the hole beneath the limb and breaking your leg. Nigel's men were upon you in a moment."

He didn't know what to say. He fingered the end of her braid and wondered at the emotions swirling inside him. "You could've told me."

"I had to be sure the hole was covered," she said with a shrug. "How did you know I was out here?"

"Lilacs," he murmured, becoming lost in her eyes.

"Lilacs?"

He nodded. "I followed it to you."

"And you let the darkness take over."

Aye, he had, and he would do it again if it meant he would save her. She'd become more precious to him than the salvation of his soul. "I would do it again."

Her hands cupped his face, a slight curve to her lips. "Thank you."

Unable to help himself, Cade drew her against him and claimed her lips. This time the kiss was slow, sensual and held all the dreams of a future he wished he could have with her. His body, still pulsing with desire, heated at the merest touch from her.

She moaned into his mouth, and his balls tightened. If he didn't get control of himself, he would take her again, regardless of who might come upon them or the danger that surrounded them.

He ended the kiss, and she laid her head on his chest. Cade rested his chin atop her head, content to just hold her. He had shared more with her than any other person in years. It was a good thing he was going to die, because he wouldn't be able to go a day without seeing or touching his witch.

"Phineas is dead," she murmured.

Cade felt the anguish in her words. "I'm sorry. I know how much he meant to you."

"He died sometime after midnight."

"Was he ill before you left?"

She shook her head. "He was in decent health for a man his age."

Cade stroked her back. His death must have come as quite a shock to her. He wondered how Drogan was handling the news. Phineas had been a father figure to Drogan as well, especially once Drogan's father died.

"I didn't know Phineas, but Drogan spoke very highly of him," Cade said. "Drogan often wondered how two men of the same blood could be as different as his uncle and his father."

She sighed. "I never really knew Drogan's father, but Phineas was a good man."

Cade wondered if she would say the same about him. She might have said it to him before, but was it something she said to make him feel better? Did she think highly of him to tell others he was a good man when he was gone?

He wasn't sure why he was so concerned about it. It shouldn't matter. Yet he found he wanted her to think he was a good man. He wanted her to respect him, to love him. His fingers jerked. He wasn't sure where that thought had come from, but once it had been let loose, he found he desperately wanted her love.

Do you love her?

He cared a great deal about her. He had never worried over someone like he did her. He craved her touch, her nearness. He dreamt of her and of a future they could have had together if things were different.

He yearned to see her belly swell with his child, to stand with her through the years as their children grew. He wanted to see her fiery locks turn silver. He wanted her eyes to be the last thing he saw before he took his final breath.

Whether that was love or not, he wasn't sure.

"I need to get you back to Adrianna before she becomes worried," he said into her hair.

Francesca lifted her head and looked at him. "I hate saying good-bye to you. These past two days have been awful. Please, come to the castle. Let me see you, be near you. Eat with us and lay your head upon a feather pillow instead of the hard ground."

It was tempting, especially since he knew being around her calmed the darkness and gave him peace, but he couldn't chance hurting anyone.

"I cannot."

She blew out a breath and stepped out of his arms. "You're a stubborn man, Cade."

"I know. Come. Let me take you back to Adrianna." He held out his hand for her.

When she placed her hand in his, a small thrill went through him. How such a small touch, so simple a gesture could affect him so, he didn't know. But he was glad of it.

Chapter Twenty-one

All too soon, Cade led Francesca to Adrianna. It had felt so good, so right to have him hold her. Francesca hadn't meant to tell him of Phineas, but her pain was still too new and raw to be held back. Cade's arms had tightened a fraction, squeezing her close so she knew he understood her pain. Being with Cade, for however short a time, gave her added strength.

He had given into the darkness, again. For her. To save her. He had jeopardized his desire to battle Nigel by letting the evil out, unsure if he could pull it back in again.

Drina rolled her eyes when she spotted them walking towards her. She didn't say anything, just raised her brows.

"No more sneaking out of the castle," Cade said to her before he glanced at Adrianna. "If you have another vision, I'd rather you come to me than to attempt something like this again."

Adrianna gasped. "There's blood on you, Fran."

"It's not mine," she hurried to assure her.

"There was an attack," Cade explained. "Nigel sent scouts who happened upon my witch."

Francesca bit her lip to keep from smiling. *My witch*, he'd called her. Aye, she was most certainly his. For now and forever.

"Are you hurt?" Adrianna asked.

Francesca shook her head. "Cade arrived in time to save me."

"Which is why there cannot be anyone else leaving the castle."

Cade glanced back the way they had come. "Nigel will arrive soon. Very soon. I feel it in my bones."

Francesca agreed with him, but she kept silent.

Adrianna looked around the woods. "We need to get back, Fran. We've been gone far longer than we should."

"I'll keep watch until you're through the wall," Cade told her. "Now go."

Francesca leaned up on her toes and gave him a quick kiss. "Stay safe."

In an instant, a magic haze surrounded her eyesight. Just like when she dreamed, she knew magic had taken her. She saw Cade, the sun shining upon his golden head. He turned and looked over his shoulder and smiled at someone. In his gaze, she saw desire and...love.

She released him and stumbled back. His hands caught her, steadying her.

"What is it?" he asked.

Francesca swallowed. Never before had her visions come to her when she was awake, but she knew she was seeing Cade's future. She should be happy that he would survive Nigel's attack. Why, then, did it hurt so desperately to know he was with someone else?

"Witch?"

She blinked and shook her head. "Nothing. I'm just weary."

She turned and hurried past Adrianna before she gave in to her heart and stayed with Cade. She was shaken to her very core at what had happened. Her magic had grown. Drastically. Nigel would arrive in days, and there were things she had to get in order first. She could feel Cade's eyes on her, could still taste him on her tongue, could still feel him between her legs.

She dreaded Nigel coming, but at least once he arrived, she wouldn't have long to agonize over Cade and what could have been.

"Fran," Drina whispered as she rushed to catch up with her. She took Francesca hand in her own and gave it a squeeze. "What happened?"

"Too much. Not enough."

They reached the postern door, and when she pulled, it came open. Francesca glanced at the woods to find Cade watching her, an unreadable expression on his face. She lifted her hand in a wave. She knew in her heart it would be the last time she saw him.

As soon as he raised his hand in return, she walked through the door. Once in the bailey, Adrianna shut and bolted the door.

Francesca leaned against the castle wall. "I never saw Cade in my future."

"Love is like that," Drina said. "It comes when you least expect it. You said we'd win against Nigel. Surely there is a future for you and Cade."

Francesca didn't have the heart to argue. "Maybe."

"What happened in the forest? When you touched Cade?"

"My powers have grown. I saw into his future."

Adrianna's brows rose. "With just a touch?"

"With just a touch. I wasn't even trying. It just...happened."

"What did you see?"

Francesca lowered her gaze to the ground as she recalled the happiness reflected in his smile and the love mirrored in his eyes. "He was happy."

Adrianna wrapped an arm around her. "We'll get through this, Fran."

Francesca let Drina lead her back into the castle. When they walked into the great hall, they found Grayson pacing in front of the empty hearth, his hands fisted at his side.

As soon as he saw Adrianna, he rushed towards her. Francesca watched her fly into her husband's arms. She had never thought about love and marriage before, but since meeting Cade, that was all she seemed to think about.

She was angry that she was the one having the sacrifice her life for the others. They had their happiness. Why couldn't she? As soon as the thought flew through her mind, she regretted it. It wasn't like her to be so selfish, but that was what she became when she thought of Cade.

"Where have you been?" Grayson demanded of his wife.

Adrianna glanced at Francesca over her shoulder. "I've been with Fran. She's grieving, Grayson, and she needed a friend."

The way Grayson looked into Adrianna's eyes, Francesca could tell he knew his wife lied, but he let her. He whispered something in her ear, and she nodded.

To have that kind of trust, that kind of relationship with someone, was astonishing to Francesca. All her life, she hadn't thought it possible for a *bana-bhuidseach* to find happiness with a man that lasted, but the two women with her proved her wrong.

Francesca walked toward the hearth and overheard Grayson whisper Cade's name and curse. Adrianna glanced at her. Francesca couldn't blame her for telling her husband what had transpired—she just hoped Grayson kept it to himself.

"No one was hurt," Adrianna murmured.

Grayson cursed again. "You could've been."

"I wasn't."

Grayson swallowed, his expression pained. "I cannot lose you, Drina. You are my life."

You are my life.

Grayson's words echoed in Francesca's mind. She knew exactly how he felt, for the mere thought of losing Cade made her chest feel empty and her heart like it was shattered into a million pieces.

Francesca resumed the seat she had vacated earlier when Drogan asked her to accompany him. It was almost as if the past hour hadn't occurred, as if she hadn't just been in Cade's arms and felt his cock deep inside her.

She placed her hand over her stomach. As often as they had made love, there was a distinct possibility she was pregnant. It should have sent her into hysterics, yet she found the thought soothing and right.

It can't be right if I'm going to die.

As much as she found herself suddenly wanting Cade's child, she knew she wasn't pregnant. It would be a cruel twist of fate. Already she had cursed fate for giving her Cade only to have him taken from her.

Francesca took a deep, steadying breath and turned her head—to find Serena and Adrianna watching her. Adrianna motioned with her head toward the stairs, and Francesca had no choice but to follow. She trailed after Serena and Adrianna, and once they were out of earshot of the men, the two women faced her.

"What has happened?" Serena asked. "You look...different."

Francesca wanted to roll her eyes.

"Her powers have grown," Drina answered.

Serena's brows lifted. "What?"

Francesca shrugged. "I touched Cade and saw a glimpse into his future."

"You've never done that before. Have you?" Serena asked.

"Nay. My visions have only ever come in my dreams."

Adrianna put her hands on her hips. "Could it be the darkness? She's been with Cade a large part of the past several days."

"It's not the darkness," Francesca argued.

Serena's brow furrowed. "Are you sure?"

"Tell her," Adrianna urged. "Tell her what you told me of the visions."

Francesca sighed and briefly closed her eyes. "I've seen the battle."

"I figured as much," Serena said. "It was the look in your eyes every time Drogan brought it up."

"You never said anything."

Serena lifted one shoulder in a shrug. "I'm not the one with visions, Fran. I assumed you had a good reason for not telling us."

Adrianna leaned against the wall. "She does. Or did."

"You cannot tell your husbands," Francesca said. "In my vision, we win the battle over Nigel, but everything must stay on its present course."

Serena nodded. "I agree. As much as I know Drogan would love this information, we cannot chance Nigel winning. He must be defeated. I'm tired of Drogan's sleepless nights as he worries over our safety."

"Nigel will die," Francesca promised. She had seen it for years. Regardless that her visions had changed and fear had taken hold of her, she could not let Nigel live. For the sake of her friends and Cade, she would kill Nigel.

Adrianna's blue eyes shifted to her. "I hope you're right, Fran."

"My visions have never been wrong."

"We keep this to ourselves," Serena said. "As for your magic increasing, Fran, I don't know what that means."

Francesca did, though. It meant that she was preparing for Nigel. And he was close.

"Could it be Cade?" Adrianna suggested.

She blew out a breath, frustration and weariness giving way. "It's not his darkness," Francesca ground out.

Serena shook her head. "That's not what Drina means. I think she's talking about what has developed between you and Cade."

Francesca remained silent.

"It could be," Adrianna said, "though my powers didn't increase when I fell in love with Grayson."

"Nor mine with Drogan," Serena agreed. "There's something different here, that's for sure."

Chapter Twenty-two

Cade came awake instantly, his knives in his hand. The fire had dwindled to a small flame, but it gave enough light for him to see he was alone.

He blew out a breath, hating the disappointment that he hadn't opened his eyes to see Francesca. He'd been dreaming of her, of that strange look that had passed over her tawny eyes the last time she had touched him.

Her magic had flared around him, and he knew that somehow, she had glimpsed his future. It wasn't sadness, but pain he had seen her gaze. He had wanted to ask her what she saw, but she had left before he'd had time.

Had she witnessed the monster he would become once the darkness took complete control over him? She had seen the darkness overcome him, but she didn't know of the carnage he would leave behind when he gave into it.

Cade sat up and sheathed his knives at his back. Dawn streaked the sky, gray giving way to pinks and oranges. The darkness had taunted him all night, alternating between begging and urging.

He splashed water on his face and grabbed an oatcake before walking to the mouth of the cave. The sound of the waves crashing onto shore in the silence of the dawn was one of Cade's favorites.

Once he finished his morning meal, he sat on a rock and began to sharpen his weapons. Cade had just sheathed his dagger after wiping it down when he felt the ground tremble.

He shot to his feet, his gaze turned to the forest.

"You've finally come," Cade murmured.

Now his redemption was close at hand. He hurried to the woods, blending with the trees. Red hazed his vision, but he pushed against the darkness. It wasn't time to unleash the monster yet. Nigel's army was still a ways off yet, but when they arrived, he would be ready for them.

An image of Francesca flashed in his mind. He'd vowed to keep her from harm, and Cade refused to break that promise. He would find and kill Nigel.

For her.

His witch.

Mine.

All of Cade's hatred and anger centered on Nigel. He had lost everything because of Nigel, all because Cade had been good with a blade.

Cade had no illusions that he wouldn't go to Hell. It was where he belonged after all the sins he had committed. But he would make sure Nigel wasn't around to do any more harm before Cade gave his soul up to the devil.

He closed his eyes and pictured Francesca.

Just thinking of her soothed him, eased the darkness within him. She was all that was good and pure in the world, and he had dared to touch her, to tarnish her with his stained soul.

He glanced at the castle, wishing for one more glimpse of her, to see her fiery locks blowing in the breeze. He said a silent thanks to God for giving him a few days with Francesca. It wasn't enough, but even an eternity with her wouldn't be enough.

Cade wondered if she would marry. The thought of another man touching her made him clench his fist. Yet she was a woman who deserved some happiness, deserved to be loved.

He wished he could be the man to give her that love. His mother would have loved Francesca, and his sisters would have brought her into the family quickly. Even his brother and father would've liked her.

"Enough," he murmured and turned back to the forest.

Nigel was on the march. His men would be in view soon, and Cade's blades would be covered in blood before the day was out.

But by sundown, Nigel would be dead.

* * * * *

Francesca's heart dropped to her feet. Nigel and his army would soon surround Wolfglynn. She had woken in the middle of the night after another dream of the blackness swallowing her, Nigel's laughter echoing around her.

She hadn't wanted to chance sleep again. With the first rays of the sun, she had rose and dressed, with the feeling that today was the day never far from her mind.

And then the distant rumbling began.

The knights in the bailey had hurried to prepare. The people of Wolfglynn rushed to hide while babies screamed and women cried silent tears and the evil descended over the castle. Francesca hadn't left her chamber yet. She had stood at her window, staring at the forest. Cade, she knew, was in the woods waiting for Nigel.

Only Nigel wouldn't be in the trees.

She took a deep breath and wondered how long she had before it was time to face Nigel and her destiny. This day had been coming for so long, and she had thought she would be ready, that she could face it with dignity and strength.

Now she wasn't so sure.

Fear clouded her mind and froze her blood. As she turned to look at the grassy hill where she and Nigel would battle, she felt a jolt of panic. Francesca jumped when someone pounded on her door. Before she could tell the person to enter, her door flew open. She turned to find Serena.

"He's here."

Francesca nodded. "I know."

"Are you sure, Fran? You saw us defeat Nigel?"

Francesca forced a smile.

"Will anything happen to Drogan?" Serena asked, wringing her hands. "I don't know what I'd do if something happened to him."

"Then keep him in the castle. No matter what you have to do, keep him behind the gates."

Serena licked her lips. "Drogan wants me and our son in the secret chamber now."

"I agree."

"There is much I can do yet. My people are frightened and looking for reassurance."

Francesca walked to take Serena's hands in hers. "Then give it to them by remaining calm and confident. We will win this day."

Serena smiled and nodded. "Aye. We'll win. Come, none of us should be alone during this."

She had no choice but to go with Serena when all Francesca wanted to do was hide in her chamber and try to ready herself for the battle with Nigel. No matter how hard she tried, though, all she could think about was Cade and whether he was all right. She wished he was with her so she could give him one last kiss, feel his arms about her one more time.

As soon as she and Serena walked down the stairs into the great hall, she spotted Grayson and Cade with other knights, giving orders. Both men had on chainmail between their tunics and leather jerkins, but they had opted against armor.

"What now?" Adrianna asked as she walked up with the infant in her arms.

Serena took her sleeping son into her arms and glanced at Drogan.

"We wait," Francesca said.

"My lord," a knight bellowed as he rushed into the hall. "We've spotted them."

Francesca clasped her hands behind her back so no one would see how they trembled. Drogan glanced at the three of them before he nodded to the knight.

"I want no one visible for this sack of wine," Drogan said. "Keep everyone out of sight and quiet."

The knights hurried to carry out his order. It wouldn't be long before he made sure they were all secured in the secret chamber. Francesca would somehow have to escape unseen. If Drogan or anyone else prevented her from meeting Nigel, the outcome would be disastrous.

* * * * *

Cade waited in the trees until Nigel's men were past him. He jumped on the last man, snapping his neck in one fluid motion.

The others whirled around. He unsheathed his knives and motioned them to him. "What are you waiting for?"

"Milord forbids it," one man said, his lanky brown hair all but covering his face.

Cade shrugged. "That's too bad."

The group did nothing to stop his attack as he cut his way through the army, leaving men lying dead upon the ground one by one. The darkness cackled with glee each time blood coated his weapons. Cade didn't try to tamp the evil down. He needed it this day.

"Nigel!" he bellowed.

When Cade reached the next group, he noticed the men were different, brawnier and with stronger swords than the ones he had just killed. A red haze began to fall over his eyes, and this time when he attacked, the army fought him.

With each thrust and swing of his knives, Cade could feel the darkness growing, swallowing him. He didn't slow, didn't stop bellowing for Nigel.

The bastard had to hear him. He had to come and face Cade sometime. Even if Cade had to work his way through Nigel's entire army, he would get him.

"More. More," the darkness screamed. *"I need more blood, more death to feed me!"*

Cade was powerless to stop, even if he wanted to. He thought of nothing but Nigel as he continued to slaughter the men around him. A few managed to draw his blood, but other than the initial sting, Cade felt nothing.

The attack changed again. This time, instead of fighting against him, they seemed to hold him off. No longer were men falling dead at his feet. They stayed just out of range of his knives, gathering around him in a circle to keep him blocked in.

He almost smiled. Nigel was coming.

Chapter Twenty-three

Francesca sat beside Serena while Adrianna paced in front of them. Drogan and Grayson had left to take a look at the army from the battlements. They had been gone far longer than any of them anticipated.

The longer Francesca waited, the more her anxiety grew. Would she be able to walk out of the gates? Would she have the courage to face Nigel?

Would she falter?

She tried to remain calm, to visualize her visions where she had defeated Nigel, but with every passing heartbeat, it became more and more difficult until she gave up all together.

Drogan rushed into the hall toward Serena. He gripped her shoulders as she stood, their son in her arms. "Take our son and get to the chamber."

"Drogan...."

He shook his head. "There's not time. Cade is already attacking Nigel's army."

Francesca heart skipped a beat. Already? Cade had already attacked?

Drogan kissed his son's forehead and then Serena. "I love you."

"I love you," she whispered, tears shining in her eyes.

Francesca stood on shaky legs while Grayson and Adrianna hugged and whispered. When Adrianna finally stepped back, there were tears on her cheeks. These people were the only family Francesca had. She would not see them fall to Nigel's evil. Regardless of what she wanted, what she craved, she would fulfill her destiny. They were worth it.

Cade was worth it.

"Bar the door," Grayson said.

Drogan nodded. "With wood and magic. Don't open for anyone but us."

"Stay safe," Serena said.

And with that, the men were gone. Francesca looked around the great hall at the other women and children who would not be locked inside a protected chamber.

"We protected the castle," Serena said as if sensing her thoughts.

Francesca licked her lips. "Aye."

"Let's go," Adrianna said.

Francesca followed the other two down the stairs to the dungeon and the chamber they had prepared. While the other two went inside, Francesca gathered a bucket of fresh water and brought it to them.

She set it inside the doorway and looked at the two women who were her sisters of magic. "I'm glad I got to know both of you. For the longest time, I thought I was the last of our kind."

Adrianna gave a half-smile. "We all thought we were the last."

"What's going on?" Serena asked, her brow furrowed.

Francesca wanted to tell them, and for a moment she almost did. She swallowed and said instead, "We all have a destiny. Mine awaits me."

"Fran, what are you talking about?" Adrianna asked.

Serena rose from her seat and handed her son to Drina. Then she faced Francesca, her gaze steady. "I knew you've been keeping something from us. I thought it was because it would help the men, but now I suspect it was because of something you planned."

Francesca almost laughed. "I haven't planned anything. It's been planned for me since the day of my birth. I've been having visions of Nigel and his defeat since I was ten summers. I've known this day was coming for years, and I've prepared for it."

Adrianna's face was lined with confusion. "Fran."

Serena took a step towards her, but Francesca had been smart enough to stay at the door.

"Sit down and tell us about the visions. What part do you think you have to play?" Serena asked.

Francesca smiled a genuine smile. "Tell Cade that I...I love him."

"Tell him yourself," Serena said.

"I wish you both the very best."

As she turned to go, Serena reached out and grabbed her hand. Francesca knew she was trying to see her death, which was Serena's power. Francesca jerked her hand away and slammed the door closed. She shoved a chair beneath the handle to keep them inside long enough for her to meet Nigel.

* * * * *

Anger consumed Cade. Where was Nigel? Why wasn't the bastard coming for him?

The darkness was easier to control, as if it knew Cade would eventually let it out. He stopped trying to fight the men and took a good look at them. Their eyes held no emotion, no life. It was as if they were just bodies. And then he realized Nigel must have their souls.

Men who craved power readily gave their souls to Nigel in exchanged for strength and command. It always amazed Cade how easily men offered their souls, forever damning themselves to a life of darkness and fire. An eternal life of Hell.

It was these men whom Nigel drew his power from. He might have sold his soul to the devil, but he got his strength from others' souls. Cade plunged his knives into one of the soulless men's chest. He had moved so quickly the men hadn't had time to react. They bellowed their rage at seeing one of their own down.

Once more Cade found himself fighting, but this time, the men coming at him were just as strong, just as fast as he himself. They felt no pain, no fear. But they died just the same.

Cade ducked a vicious swing at his head only to feel a blade slash across his back. He hissed in pain but continued fighting. He moved around the circle, sinking his blades into as many bodies as he could. When one grabbed him about the neck, Cade threw back his head, slamming into the man's nose. There was a bellow, and then Cade was released.

The men's swords and axes were long, which meant Cade had to move closer to get his blades within reach of them. But it felt so good when his weapons sunk into their bodies.

"You were born to be a killer, Cade," the darkness whispered, its tone beguiling. *"Look at what you can do. Take the power I offer, and we'll conquer the world."*

Cade hated the evil, hated the way it knew what to say when he was deep in battle. He'd always been good at fighting, had always picked up the skill of a new weapon easily. His mother had said God gave gifts to people for them to use.

Had God given him the ability to kill so easily because he wanted him to do it? Cade had a hard time believing that. Besides, he didn't want to be a killer.

He wanted peace.

And Francesca.

"Kill for me," the darkness urged.

It would be so easy to give in to the lure of the evil, to be caught in the false charm.

The darkness laughed. *"You're going to Hell anyway, Cade. Give in. Let me show you what we can do."*

Cade bellowed and crossed his arms as he plunged his blades into one of the soulless men's neck. He gave a yank, and the man's head rolled to the ground. He smiled, his vision covered in red. Blood dripped from his weapons to mix with the earth. Another stain upon his soul, another mark against him.

Nigel's army took a step away from Cade as if they'd just realized who—and what—he was. But it was too late. He intended to kill every last one of them.

* * * * *

Serena pushed against the door Francesca had just slammed in her face. The icy fingers of terror had wrapped around her as she'd seen Fran's death.

"Francesca! Let us out," Serena screamed. "Don't do this."

Her son began to cry in Adrianna's arms, and Adrianna walked the chamber to soothe him. "Stop it, Serena. You're scaring your son."

Serena, her hands braced on the door, dropped her head to the wood. "We have to get out."

"Tell me what just happened. Why did Fran leave us here?"

Serena blew out a breath and faced Adrianna, her heart hammering in her chest. "I saw Francesca's death when I touched her. Nigel will take her life. Today."

Drina's face drained of color. "By the saints. It all makes sense. Everything she's said, everything she's done. She's known."

"I suspect she's always known. Her visions have told her everything."

"We have to stop her."

Serena pushed against the door. "She's blocked us in somehow."

Adrianna laid the infant on one of the beds that had been brought to the chamber and went to the door. "Not for long. Push."

They strained, pushing with all their might, the door only inching open.

"Is her death painful?" Drina asked.

Serena wished she could block out the terror she saw on Francesca's face. "Aye."

"That's how we'll win against Nigel? By her death?"

"I believe so."

Drina shook her head, her blonde braid moving against her back. "I refuse to let her die."

They shoved their shoulders into the thick door, Serena's son's cries filling the chamber. Serena closed her eyes and shoved with all her might. Of a sudden, the door slid open. She caught Drina before she tumbled to the floor.

"Now we save Francesca," Adrianna said after she gained her feet. "I refuse to let one of my sisters die."

Serena picked up her son and followed Drina from the chamber. She prayed she reached Drogan in time for him to stop Francesca. If not...Serena shuddered as she recalled the horror of Fran's death.

Fran, who had just found happiness with Cade. Fran, who had come each day to help fortify the castle with magic. Fran, whose eyes held so many secrets.

She didn't deserve to die by Nigel's hand. There had to be another way to kill him. Serena stopped on the stairs.

"Adrianna," she called.

Drina halted and turned. "What is it?"

"Cade thinks he's to be the one who kills Nigel."

"But Fran thinks she's the one."

Serena kissed her son's forehead. "Cade has no idea, does he?"

"After seeing the way he looked at her, especially after he saved her again yesterday, nay."

"What?"

"Come," Adrianna said. "I'll tell you as we find Drogan."

Serena swallowed, not liking the way her stomach rolled with dread.

"I caught Fran leaving the bailey through the postern door. She told me she had to save Cade—that she'd had a vision of him being injured by a hole in the ground. So, I went with her."

"Does Grayson know?"

Drina nodded. "Aye. He's not happy with me."

"What happened?" Serena asked as they reached the hall.

"While Fran was covering the hole, some of Nigel's men attacked. Cade got there in time to save her. The intensity of his gaze, the look of utter devotion and regret in his eyes broke my heart. He wants to protect her. If he knew what she planned, he'd chain in her in the dungeon."

Serena grimaced as they made their way through the throng of people and out of the castle. "Aye, I believe he would. Apparently Fran knew this as well, which is why she never told him."

"There's Drogan," Adrianna said once they reached the bailey.

Serena followed her finger to the battlements. "Take my son and look for Francesca. Surely she hasn't left yet.

Chapter Twenty-four

Francesca walked to the gate and the four men who guarded it. "Open the door," she commanded.

They shared a glance before the one nearest to her spoke. "I'm sorry, milady, but I cannot. Lord Drogan forbids anyone from leaving."

"Do you want to die?"

He shook his head.

"That is what's going to happen if you don't let me out. There is a man so full of evil that he will take you one at a time. I can stop him."

The guard looked at his three friends. "I don't want to die, milady, but I don't know if I believe you can kill such a man."

Francesca smiled before she reached out to touch his arm. Instantly, her magic surrounded her. She saw him surrounded by seven children as he sat by a fire, a woman humming in the background.

She dropped her hand. "You're going to have seven children and a loving wife who likes to hum."

"God's teeth," the guard swore. "You're talking about Mary. I've had my eye on her for awhile."

"Then don't wait to claim her. Now, please. Open the door."

The guard took a deep breath and reluctantly unbolted the door in the gate. Francesca stepped through, and just before he closed it, she spotted Serena and Adrianna on the castle steps.

They had gotten out faster than she had wanted, but at least she was outside the castle walls. Now, she could face her destiny and free everyone from Nigel's hold. Drogan's life could return to normal, and Cade could return to his lands and resume his life.

Francesca made herself step away from the gate. The first step was the hardest, but after she put some distance between herself and safety, it got easier to face what was ahead of her. She stayed near the wall, letting her fingers run along the gray stones as she walked to the front of the castle where the battle with Nigel would take place.

If she had her wish, no one but Nigel's army would be there to witness the battle. Drogan and the others would be watching, she was sure of it. By now, Serena would have found Drogan and told him what she was planning. But it was too late for anyone to stop her.

Nigel's army filled the space between the castle and the forest, leaving a good two hundred strides between the front line and her. Whereas usually the rolling hills were filled with running children and knights training, this time, there was an army. They stretched as far as she could see, just as had been foretold in her vision.

Francesca stopped and put her back to the castle wall. Her gaze moved to her left and the forest where Drogan had said Cade was already fighting. She could see a mass of Nigel's soldiers gathered together, and she could only hope that Cade had released the darkness and was slaughtering all that was around him.

Movement out of the corner of her eye caused her to look away from the woods. The army parted, and down their flanks rode a man on horseback. He was cloaked with his hood up, hiding his face.

But she knew it was Nigel. She could feel his evil gaze on her.

* * * * *

"Drogan!"

He spun around when he heard his wife shout his name. She was supposed to be in the secret chamber. He strode towards her as she climbed the stairs to the battlements. "What in the name of all that's holy are you doing up here?" he demanded.

She took his hands, and he felt hers shaking. He knew instantly something very bad had happened.

"What is it?" he asked.

She swallowed, her eyes filling with tears. "It's Francesca."

"Is she hurt?"

"Nay," she said with a shake of her head. "She locked me and Drina in the chamber so she could leave. To face Nigel herself. Drogan, I saw her death. Nigel kills her."

Drogan felt as if a horse had just kicked him in the stomach. Francesca might be a grown woman, but she was his responsibility now that Phineas was dead. He was supposed to protect her. "Where is she?"

"There," Grayson said.

Drogan glanced over his shoulder to see Grayson pointing on the other side of the wall. He walked to Grayson and looked over to see Francesca.

"God's blood. She's going to get herself killed," Grayson murmured.

Serena came to Drogan's other side. "She thinks her death will end Nigel. She says she's been having visions of this day since she was a little girl."

Drogan ran a hand down his face. "I have to get her."

"What of Cade?" Grayson asked.

Drogan glanced to the trees. Cade had asked him to protect Francesca. He would fail his friend again. This time, Cade would never forgive him.

"I have to go," he said.

Serena grasped his hand. "Wait," she whispered.

Drogan halted and spotted a rider coming towards Francesca. "Shite," he ground out.

It was too late. Nigel had arrived.

* * * * *

Francesca stood still, her body never betraying the fear that turned her blood to ice and made her break into a cold sweat.

The solid white horse Nigel rode clashed with his black soul. He stopped the mount midway between her and the army and dismounted. He wore no weapons, but with the power he commanded, he didn't need a sword.

Nigel slapped the horse on the rear and sent him galloping back toward his army. For a moment, he simply stood and regarded her. Francesca was amazed at the silence of Wolfglynn and the army. Not even the birds sang. When Nigel started toward her, she could hear his boots crunching on the ground.

The only other sound she heard was the battle in the woods. She recognized Cade's voice as he bellowed. He was still alive, still fighting. She almost smiled at that small victory.

If she somehow failed with Nigel, it would be up to Cade to kill him, but she hoped it didn't come to that. Cade deserved his vengeance, but he also deserved some happiness and a future bright with possibility.

"Well, well, well," Nigel said as he neared. "I've seen you in my dreams often enough."

Francesca moved away from the wall and turned her back to the trees so she could face Nigel. When he had attacked Drogan before, he had come alone and been in a suit of armor. Now, the only thing hiding him was a cloak.

She knew his eyes, though. They were small, black, and full of malice and evil. One could become lost in the hatred of Nigel's eyes if they weren't careful.

"You think you can defeat me?" Nigel taunted.

"I know I can."

"Ah. Courage. It's such a paltry thing when faced with my power. How soon do you think you'll crumble?"

"I won't," she said with more conviction than she felt.

Nigel lifted his arms and threw back the hood of his cloak. His gaze bore into hers. The black soulless eyes staring at her weren't human. The body may have been what was left of Nigel's tall, lanky form, but there was no soul inside him, only evil.

"Let's see, shall we?"

Francesca grinned. Nigel's hawkish features were difficult to look upon. As foul a person as he was, she couldn't imagine the king ever trusting him.

"Is something amusing, witch?"

Her smile faded. Cade had called her witch, never using her name, but he had made it sound like an endearment. Whereas Nigel saying it made her sound dirty and...evil.

She lifted her chin. "You are."

"Why is that?"

"It's obvious why you sold your soul."

He crossed his arms over his chest and glanced up at the wall. "You know nothing of me."

"It wasn't just power that made you sell your soul, Nigel. You could get nothing on your own. Not even women."

His lips pulled back in a sneer as he dropped his arms. "Don't pretend to know me, witch. You, who've had it all."

"You're days are numbered."

"I think not. You may think you have power. For a witch. Yet it's nothing compared to mine."

He was right, Francesca knew, but she had something to fight for. She had Drogan, Serena and their child. She had

Adrianna and Grayson. And she had Cade. They were her family.

Nigel only had his need for power. She had seen firsthand what love could do when Serena had died and Drogan had brought her back. Francesca had used all the herbs she knew, had even tried her magic, but it had been Drogan's love that brought Serena back to him.

"I can break the curse," Nigel said.

Francesca jerked.

Nigel smiled and nodded. "Aye, I know of the curse. I know all there is to know about you, Francesca. It's a pity Phineas wasn't able to last longer."

A pang of pain shot through her. "You killed Phineas."

"He was old—it was his time to go."

She had known Phineas wasn't sick. "He had done nothing to you."

Nigel shrugged. "I wanted to kill something, so I killed Phineas. It's as simple as that."

Hate began to boil within her. She wanted to tear Nigel limb from limb, to see his blood leach from his body and his bones decay into nothing.

"Aye, Francesca, let the hate grow. How do you think I got Cade under my control?"

She'd wondered when he would bring up Cade, but now that he had, she wished he hadn't. She couldn't think about Cade or anything else other than Nigel. She had to keep her focus or she would fail.

"I'll kill you and the other witches. By the time I'm done at Wolfglynn, Cade will be mine to control."

She shook her head. "He was never yours to control, and he never will be. He will fight the darkness. And he will win."

"Without you, witch, Cade will descend into the evil and never return."

He lifted his hands, palm up, and a blast of power shot towards her.

Francesca closed her eyes and lifted her own hands in defense, expecting to feel Nigel's evil surround her. Only there was nothing. She opened her eyes to find white light pouring from her hands.

In all her visions, she thought the light had come from Nigel. Her magic pulsed inside her, beating with her heart and growing stronger with each breath. She opened herself up to the magic, gave in to its need to be released.

She was going to beat Nigel. She would be the one to end his life and free his reign over everyone. The fear that had encased her heart in ice disappeared and left her with a confidence and strength she'd never known before.

A smile pulled at her lips as her magic grew and overshadowed his evil. He faltered, his brows furrowing as he realized she was stronger than he had expected.

"All of you fell into my trap."

She raised her brows. "How is that?"

"Everyone thought I wanted Drogan or Gerard, when all I wanted was Cade. I could have killed Drogan easily. The same with Grayson."

Francesca's smile dropped.

"You gave Cade hope, something he hasn't had in years. When that hope is dead, he will no longer fight the darkness within him. He will be mine."

"You lie." She couldn't trust him. Nigel was evil and would spout evil to get what he wanted.

"Can you feel it, witch? Can you feel the shift of power as Cade realizes you failed him?"

Francesca sucked in a breath.

Nigel began to laugh, and she realized too late he had tricked her. As soon as she had taken her attention off him, he had overpowered her. His evil surrounded her, blanketing her in blackness.

Dimly, she heard someone scream and realized it had been her, screaming for Cade.

Chapter Twenty-five

Drogan's arms wrapped around Serena as she buried her head in his chest, her hand over her mouth. He could hardly believe what he'd seen. Francesca had nearly beaten Nigel, but the bastard had said something to her which caused her to lose her concentration.

And Drogan knew Nigel had spoken of Cade.

He glanced at the forest to see the army, their weapons still drawn, but silent as they circled something. Cade was still alive. Nigel glanced at Drogan again before he strode back to his army.

"You have to get her," Serena said as she raised her face to him. "Don't leave her out there."

"I'm not."

He set Serena away from him and motioned his best knights forward. When he stood at the gate, Grayson was beside him.

"Until the end," Grayson said.

"Until the end." He glanced at his men. "Just make sure Grayson and I aren't attacked. Don't look at them," he cautioned.

The knights mumbled agreement, and with a nod from Drogan, the guards cracked open the gates. As soon as they were through, the gates closed behind them.

Drogan rushed around the castle to where Francesca lay in the grass, the sun shining down upon her. He lifted her in his arms as Grayson stood beside him, his sword drawn.

"Go," Grayson said.

Drogan half-ran, half-walked back to the gates. He expected Nigel to attack, but there was nothing.

"That was odd," Grayson said when they were once more inside the bailey. "He had the perfect opportunity to kill us."

"I don't think it's us he wants."

Serena and Adrianna were by their side in an instant. Serena brushed a lock of Francesca's red hair from her face. "Where is she wounded?"

"I see no wound," Grayson said.

Adrianna, holding the infant, leaned close. "She breathes still. I can heal her if we hurry."

"Get her to her chamber," Serena said.

Drogan followed his wife into the castle, all the while wishing Cade was with him. Cade needed to know about Fran, but more than that, Fran needed Cade.

* * * * *

Cade swung his knives around him, his gaze moving from face to face. The darkness inside him hungered for blood, but Cade held it off. It wasn't time yet. Nigel hadn't shown himself. Suddenly, the men around him stepped back, widening the circle and parting. The darkness reared its head, sensing the evil that approached.

Nigel.

As soon as he saw his nemesis, Cade's vision went red. He'd been waiting for the day when he could battle Nigel and end the malevolence that had gripped the land.

"Hello, Cade," Nigel said as he stopped and the circle closed around him.

Cade peeled back his lips in a sneer. There would be no time wasted on talking. It was time for dying, and Cade was the one who would be taking Nigel's life this day.

"It's been a long time."

Cade narrowed his gaze. "Enough talking. Fight me."

"Not yet," Nigel said and crossed his arms over his chest.

"Aye. Now."

Nigel chuckled and shook his head. "You always were so stubborn. If only you had let me take control of you long ago, you wouldn't have had to suffer as you have these last years."

"Could it be that you're afraid to fight me?" Cade taunted. "The mighty Baron Nigel Creely, who sold his soul to Satan."

Nigel's face mottled red. "I could take your soul now."

Cade could barely stand to look at the narrow face and beady eyes. He had hated Nigel from the first moment he'd seen him, and the hate had only grown over the years.

"It's an empty threat," he told Nigel. "If you could have taken my soul, you'd have done it already."

Nigel took a deep breath, his features once more serene and emotionless. "I'm more powerful than you think."

"I've seen your power, but I don't think it's as great as you'd like everyone to believe. If you could take anyone's soul, why haven't you taken Drogan's?"

"Ah, Drogan," Nigel said and dropped his arms. "I wondered when you would get around to him. I'll explain it to you as I did Francesca."

Cade jerked when he heard her name. "When did you talk to her?"

A slow, evil smile filled Nigel's face. "Just a few moments ago, actually. She didn't fare so well, I'm afraid."

The darkness bellowed within him, but it wasn't for blood, it was for his witch. Cade whipped around and pushed through the men surrounding him. He spotted Drogan and Grayson and a lock of red hair before they disappeared around the castle wall.

Fear took root in Cade's stomach and clawed at him, aligning with the darkness and demanding revenge, demanding blood. Nigel's blood.

"Do you want to know what happened?" Nigel whispered behind him.

Cade spun around, his blade at Nigel's throat. "I could kill you now."

"Nay, you couldn't. Before you do something so foolish, though, I advise you to pay a visit to your witch. Then we'll talk."

Nigel disappeared as soon as the last words left his lips. Cade stared at the now empty spot, feeling lost and unsure. Francesca was hurt, of that he knew. But how badly?

The red haze was gone, replaced with the knowledge that he might have lost Francesca.

She was never yours.

But she could have been. She'd wanted to be. And he'd lost her. What a fool he'd been. The best thing that had ever happened to him, he hadn't held on to.

You couldn't. You still can't.

It was true. He had no right to hold on to Francesca. His life was coming to an end. What, exactly, Nigel was up to he didn't know yet. But he intended to find out.

Cade wiped off his weapons and sheathed them as he made his way out of the forest to the castle. With every step, his mind screamed at him to stop, that he couldn't enter the gates. Anything could set the darkness off, and Cade would kill everyone.

But he had to take the chance. For Francesca.

My witch.

He glanced at Nigel's men who surrounded the castle. They didn't attack, just stood ready, watching. Drogan was outnumbered five to one, and Nigel knew it. So what was Nigel's game? What did Nigel want?

Cade stopped before the tall gates. He heard someone shout Drogan's name. Out of the corner of his eye, he saw Drogan lean over the battlements before he ordered the gate opened. There was a pop as the gates were unbolted and opened far enough for him to squeeze through. Cade's chest felt tight, as if a horse sat on him, squeezing his breath, and his life, from his body.

"Cade," Drogan said as he rushed to him.

But Cade didn't have time for him. He could already smell the lilacs. He lengthened his legs until he was running. He heard Drogan behind him, but he didn't stop as he ran through the great hall and took the stairs three at a time.

He continued to follow Francesca's scent until it led him down a hallway to a door. Cade paused at the door and stared inside to see Francesca lying on the bed, her face pale and her fiery hair spread out on the pillow.

Serena stood near the bed as Adrianna tried to heal Francesca. As soon as they noticed him, they stepped away from the bed. Cade moved into the room and saw Grayson standing off to the side.

Cade knelt by the bed, his heart in his throat. He reached a hand out to touch Francesca's face, then noticed the blood and cuts on his hand. He didn't want to mar her beautiful skin with the blood, but he had to touch her.

He smoothed a lock of hair from her face and silently prayed that she would open her eyes.

"I've tried to heal her," Drina said. "I've used all my magic, but she won't open her eyes."

Serena took a step to the bed. "We can't find where she's injured, Cade."

"What happened?" he choked out.

Serena swallowed and glanced at the doorway. "She locked me and Drina in the chamber. She told us it was her destiny to kill Nigel, that she'd had visions of this day since she was a little girl."

Cade squeezed his eyes close. Why hadn't she told him?

"She was out of the castle before we reached Drogan," Adrianna said. "All we could do was watch as they walked toward each other."

"Did he speak to her?" Cade asked.

"Aye," Drogan answered. "We couldn't hear them, but they spoke."

He glanced over his shoulder at Drogan. "What happened next?"

"Nigel threw up his hands. Fran raised hers as well, and a white light began to envelop Nigel. We thought she was going to win. We could see him weakening."

"Then he said something to her," Grayson said. "She faltered, and then she screamed."

"Nigel walked away, and we rushed to get her," Drogan said.

Cade sat back on his heels and covered her hand with his, lowering his forehead to their hands. "You won't be able to wake her."

"What do you mean?" Drogan asked.

"Nigel has taken her soul."

A hand clamped on his shoulder. He didn't need to look up to know it was Drogan.

"What can we do?" Grayson asked.

"Nothing. I've seen this before. Her body will waste away as we watch. Unless her soul is returned, she'll die."

Cade took a deep breath and rose to his feet. He stared at Francesca's face, hating himself for what had happened to her, hating that he hadn't been able to protect her as he'd promised.

"We'll fight with you," Grayson said. "The bastard tried to take my soul and wasn't able to."

Cade tried to smile at Grayson. He appreciated his offer, but Cade couldn't allow anyone to come with him. "There's nothing you can do. Nigel wants me."

"Cade," Drogan said and moved to stand beside him.

Cade shook his head. "Nay. I've run long enough."

Serena took his hand. "Fran asked me to tell you something."

Just hearing her name caused his heart to skip a beat.

"She told me to tell you that she loves you."

If Cade had hurt before, it was nothing compared to the pain in his heart now. It felt as if someone had ripped him in two.

"I'll get her soul back," he vowed. "I won't let Nigel hold her."

Drogan stepped in front of him when he tried to move. "We'll figure something out, Cade. Don't give in to Nigel, not after fighting it all these years."

"Look at her," he bellowed and pointed to Francesca. "Already the color of her hair fades. He'll drain her in days, Drogan. I cannot, and will not, let that happen. He wants me."

"He's a monster."

Cade blew out a breath. "So am I. If he could have taken my soul, he'd have done it already. The darkness inside me is too great. He can't take me without my consent, regardless of how powerful he is."

He shifted his gaze from Drogan to Serena. "I was a fool. I should have told her myself that she had my heart. I won't get that chance now."

"I'll make sure she knows," Serena said, blinking back tears.

"Keep her safe, Drogan."

Drogan nodded. "You have my word."

"Once...once I give myself to Nigel, he'll send me here." It was difficult to say, much less imagine, but he knew Nigel well enough to know the bastard would enjoy two friends killing each other.

Drogan put a hand on Cade's shoulder. "I'll be prepared."

"Don't let me...." Cade couldn't even finish the sentence.

"We won't," Grayson promised as he stepped forward.

With a nod to Serena and Adrianna, he leaned down and kissed Francesca. His witch. With a sigh, he straightened and turned on his heel.

Drogan expelled a deep breath and gave a curt nod to Grayson. He didn't want to kill Cade, but he had no choice. It seemed Nigel was constantly putting them in situations where they had no choice.

"This is wrong," Adrianna said. "I sense the darkness around Cade, but I don't smell the evil as I do when Nigel and his men are around."

"It's always been wrong," Drogan said.

The haunted look on Cade's face when he'd seen Francesca lying in the bed would stay with Drogan forever. If there was ever a man who deserved happiness, it was Cade. He followed Cade out of the castle to the bailey. Everyone gave him a wide berth, shrinking in fear when he neared. Drogan glanced at his friend to see his face hardened, anger sparking in his gaze.

They stopped before the gate. Finally Cade had been inside the castle, and the only person who had managed to get him there was Francesca. His love for her went deep. It seemed unwarranted that Cade would lose his future and his life because of Nigel.

"I wish I was going with you."

Cade shook his head, his golden hair moving over his neck. "Nay. You don't. Even if I manage to beat him, the darkness will be fully unleashed."

"Francesca will be released upon his death, aye?"

"Aye."

"Then she should be able to calm you as before."

Cade shook his head, again. "Before, I thought I had let go completely, but I hadn't. This time...this time it will be for good."

Drogan swallowed, wishing there was some way he could help him.

Cade reached over his shoulders and unsheathed his knives. The blades glistened as the sun broke from behind a cloud.

Cade flipped the knives until he held them backwards, the blades following his arms.

"Remember your promise," he said as the gates opened.

"Godspeed, my brother. It was a privilege knowing you."

Cade paused and looked at Drogan. "I never deserved your friendship."

"You deserved much more than you got."

"If you knew the things I had done."

"I would still call you brother."

Cade closed his eyes and took a deep breath. When he opened them again, they were red. The darkness swirled around him, menacing and evil. He walked from Drogan, never looking back. Drogan clenched his fists, wanting to see Nigel's life drain away as he choked him. Nigel had ruined so many lives.

"Farewell. Brother," Drogan whispered as the gate closed.

Chapter Twenty-six

Francesca opened her mouth to scream as the claws tore her flesh from her body again and again. The agony was blinding, the torment relentless. She had tried to see in the blackness for some semblance of light, but there was nothing, and she gave up. She kept her eyes closed, her lips parted in a silent scream. If only she could move, make some kind of sound.

But she could hear everything. The creatures cackling with glee, the claws sinking into her skin, and the sound of her flesh tearing from her bones.

It was a nightmare she knew she would never wake from. She could go insane if she let herself. Then she would think of Cade. She imagined his vivid blue eyes gazing at her with desire. She recalled the feel of his lips upon hers and the way he stole her breath every time he kissed her. She felt his hands on her, guiding his arousal inside her.

Then she would lose herself in the pain, forgetting who she was, what she loved.

"Francesca," a voice called.

The torment stopped, and for a moment there was no pain, only the stillness around her. She recognized the voice, though.

Nigel! Then she recalled how she had failed, how he had trapped her.

"Open your eyes, Francesca," he beseeched.

She shook her head.

"Open your eyes or I'll call the hounds back." His voice had hardened, and she had no doubt he would send her back to the agony. Francesca took a deep breath and opened her eyes. Light flooded her from atop the small hill. She raised her arm to shield her eyes, only realizing then that she was able to move.

"Where am I?"

There was a chuckle beside her. She glanced over to see Nigel, still wearing the cloak, standing with his hands behind her back.

"It's lovely, is it not?"

Francesca turned her attention to the castle that stood before her. It wasn't as large as Wolfglynn, but it held impressive towers and a sturdy wall and gatehouse. The rolling hills filled with wildflowers brought a serenity to the castle, a calmness. In the distance was a small forest. A small group of men on horseback raced to the trees, following a stag.

She knew Nigel had brought her to this place to show her something, and the more she looked around at it, the more she wanted to leave. It was a beautiful place, and his presence would only destroy it.

"It's called Stonelake," he said.

She glimpsed the edge of water on the other side of the castle. "Why are we here?"

He smiled, chilling her. "I want you to see something."

Francesca blinked, and they were inside the castle in the great hall. A woman with long golden curls beginning to streak with white sat near the hearth, sewing. She had the sweetest smile, the gentlest of hands as she reached over to the girl beside her.

One glance at the two and Francesca knew they were mother and daughter. It wasn't until the daughter raised her face and she found herself staring into vivid blue eyes that she realized where they were.

Cade's home.

Two more girls came into the hall. The smallest, with a cherub face and dark blonde braids, raced after the older one, who had a mischievous smile and light brown hair.

All had the same eyes as Cade.

Francesca swallowed, afraid to watch, but unable to look away.

It was a happy scene, a family enjoying the day and the love between them. Suddenly, the door to the castle flew open. Cade stood in the doorway, his hair hanging past his shoulders and windblown. He was covered in dust with a wild look about him.

She had only to look into his eyes to see the darkness had a hold of him. A sick feeling centered in her stomach as his sisters ran to him, throwing their arms around him. They shouted his name while he stood there, his face a mask of fear and confusion.

He didn't touch them, and when they finally moved away, he walked to his mother. Her brows were furrowed, concern lining her face.

"Cade," she said and rose to her feet. "What is it? Why have you returned so soon?"

He stumbled forward, and she reached out to help him. He jerked away from her as if stung. "Don't touch me," he bellowed.

His sisters shrank away, their eyes wide with fright.

"Girls, to your chambers," his mother ordered. Once they were gone, she faced Cade. "You aren't yourself, son."

He laughed, the sound mirthless and defeated. "Nay. I'm not."

"What can I do?"

He sank into the chair near her and buried his face in his hands. "I had thought coming here would help. I was wrong."

"Cade? You're scaring me."

He lifted his face to look at her. "Run, Mother. Grab my sisters and run. Run as far away from me as you can."

"Nay. I'm your mother. I can help you."

He leapt to his feet. "No one can help me!"

A heartbeat later, he grabbed his head and fell to his knees.

His mother was at his side in an instant, her arms around him. Francesca couldn't breathe. She had a feeling she knew what was going to happen, and it broke her heart to see Cade torn apart with the darkness.

"Cade," his mother soothed and wiped his hair from his face.

When he lifted his eyes, now red, to her, she stood and backed away from him. "What have you done with my son, you devil?"

Cade's face twisted in agony. "It is me, Mother."

"Fight it, Cade. Fight it for us."

He clenched his jaw. "I can't. I'm not strong enough."

His mother took another step away from him, her face pale in fear. "I love you, Cade. Never forget that."

"Stop!" he yelled and grabbed his head again. "Please, God, stop."

Francesca couldn't tell if he was talking to the darkness or his mother. The pain he was in brought her to tears.

Slowly, he dropped his hands and lifted his head. "Please, leave," he begged.

"Nay," his mother stated. "I know you. You're strong. You can beat this."

He shook his head and unsheathed his sword. "I'm...trying."

Cade backed her into the solar. His mother stood strong, her love shining through her blue eyes. "Whatever you are inside my son, leave."

Still Cade advanced on her. He lifted his sword.

"Find a way to fight this, Cade," she said just before he sunk his sword into her.

Francesca tried to look away, but her gaze was drawn to Cade. A tear ran down his face as he turned to find his sisters in the doorway. His eyes glowed, and it was as if he lost himself to the darkness as he killed all three of them.

When the last fell, Cade stood in the solar staring at them, tears rolling down his face. His sword fell from his fingers, and he dropped to his knees, lifting the youngest in his arms. He rocked her back and forth, mumbling into her hair. There was a noise from the great hall, and when Cade looked up, there was a man in front of him.

Francesca covered her mouth with her hand. The man was younger than Cade, with his same eyes, but that was where the similarities ended. He was shorter than Cade, lithe where Cade's muscles were pronounced. His hair was a light brown, and his face held none of the appeal of Cade's.

"What have you done?" the man demanded.

Cade's eyes had begun to return to normal, but at his brother's appearance, the red once more took over. He grabbed his sword and stood.

"Cade?" his brother asked and unsheathed his sword. "You killed our family!"

His brother lunged for him. Cade easily deflected the blow. The brother lifted his arm to attack again, and Cade stepped toward him, his blade sinking through his chest.

With a grunt, his brother dropped his weapon and clung to him. "Cade?" he asked, his face a mask of confusion.

As the life drained from his brother, Cade's eyes returned to normal again. When he saw what he'd done, he removed his sword from his brother and tossed it aside. Then, one by one, he took his family out of the castle and buried them.

No one stopped him. No one helped.

Francesca couldn't stop her tears. It was no wonder Cade carried such a weight around on his shoulders. After what the darkness had made him do, it was a wonder he'd been able to get it under control.

"He should have been mine then," Nigel said.

Francesca looked away from Cade standing over the graves of his family while the sun set, back to Nigel. "You did this, didn't you?"

Nigel shrugged. "I helped."

Cade didn't return to the castle. He simply walked away, never looking back at his home or his family.

"But he wasn't yours. After killing his family, he fought the darkness. And won."

Nigel clenched his jaw. "I made sure he had nothing to return to. I burned the castle and began hunting and killing anyone Cade had ever known and loved."

"Why show me this?" she demanded.

"I want you to see what kind of power I have. I have your soul, my dear witch. I can control you forever."

She swallowed, hoping the tremor of fear that ran through her hadn't been seen. "I will fight you. Just as Cade fought the darkness."

"You are so naïve. I can control your body now. If I wanted, I could sink the darkness into you as I did with Cade, Drogan and Gerard. You aren't strong enough to overpower such evil."

"What do you want?"

"Cade," he answered without hesitation. "It won't be long before I have him either."

"Take me instead."

His smile grew. "I already have you."

"Then what do I have that I can give you in exchange for Cade?"

Nigel walked around her, eyeing her. "Your magic."

"My magic? You are powerful enough to take my soul. Why do you need my magic?"

"A son," he said, his gaze on her breasts. "I need a son."

The thought of giving herself to Nigel made her want to slit her own throat, but if it would save Cade....

"In exchange for Cade?"

He shook his head. "Cade will still be mine, but I give you my word I will release him once his duty is done."

"You aren't giving me much in return?"

"I don't have to give you anything. Your body is mine to command."

She smiled then, realizing why he needed her consent. "You can father a child off my body, but it won't have my magic. Not unless I give it freely. If you want my magic, you let Cade go. Now."

Nigel threw back his head and laughed. "I think not, witch. Once you've seen what Cade becomes, you'll beg me to take your magic in exchange for releasing him."

He snapped his fingers, and she was once more in the dark. She had taken only one breath when she heard the clink of a claw coming towards her.

Cade!

Chapter Twenty-seven

Cade stalked from Wolfglynn, his anger, frustration, and pain over failing Francesca weighing heavily upon him. He wanted Nigel's death, and though he told Drogan Francesca would be released if Nigel died, he didn't know that for a fact.

He walked to the woods. Drogan and the others would be watching, and he didn't want them to see him turn into a monster. His mother had begged him to fight the darkness, and though he'd been unable to stop the evil from taking ahold of him then, he had now brought it under control.

Ever since he'd killed his family, he had forgone any type of pleasure. He didn't deserve it. He'd been too weak to take control of the darkness. All these years, he'd waited for the chance to unleash the darkness on Nigel. Nigel had thought he could control him, Drogan and Gerard with the darkness. He'd learned too late that hadn't been the case.

It was why no others held it inside them. Nigel had learned his lesson quickly.

The darkness demanded revenge for Francesca, but Cade would deny it and himself. In order to free her, they couldn't take the chance of killing Nigel.

He would turn into the monster his family had seen the day of their deaths, and Cade prayed Drogan and Grayson took him down quickly. Once the evil was released, death was quick to follow wherever he went.

"How is she?"

Cade jerked to a stop and turned to see Nigel leaning against a tree. His powers had grown so much that he could move through space and time at will.

"You know how she is," Cade answered.

Nigel shrugged and pushed off the tree. "She'll lay there for as long as I want her to, but I don't want her wasting away. I have other plans for her...body."

Cade's vision instantly went red. He knew precisely what Nigel wanted with his witch, and he wasn't going to let that happen.

"You won't touch her," Cade said between clenched teeth.

Nigel laughed. "I'll do much more than touch her. As it is, I've been showing her some bits of your past."

It was like a bucket of ice water had been thrown on him. He knew without asking what Nigel had shown Francesca: the day he'd killed his family.

His gut twisted painfully as he imagined how Francesca had reacted. She might have professed her love of him, but after seeing what he'd done, what he'd become that fateful day, she would want no part of him.

If only he could turn his heart away from her, but he couldn't. She had touched him as no one had, given him everything without question. She had offered him paradise. The least he could do was to set her free.

"You want me, Nigel?"

The smile dropped from the baron's face. "You know I do."

"Then let Francesca go, and I'll willingly come to you."

Nigel narrowed his gaze at Cade. "If I let her go now, I can get her again."

"Nay. You leave her and all *bana-bhuidseach* alone."

"Or what?" Nigel asked. "You'll refuse? I don't think so, Cade. I've seen you with her. Your love for her will make you sacrifice yourself."

"Why do you want her?"

"You mean besides her body? I do need an heir."

Cade's mind raced. Why Francesca? Why now? And then he realized—her magic. "She won't give you her magic."

Nigel shrugged. "She will eventually."

Cade stretched his shoulders. The only way Francesca would give in would be to save him. If only there was some way to let her know Nigel would never free him.

"Trying to figure out a way to save her?" Nigel asked with a sneer. "She's doing the same thing. Well, she was. I'm sure now she's screaming in pain."

Anger exploded in Cade. Everything went red, and he launched himself at Nigel. He had to die. Nigel would never leave him or Francesca alone. Never.

Cade's weapons moved with lightning speed. He attacked so quickly, Nigel didn't have a chance at escape. Again and again, Cade cut into Nigel. Every howl of pain brought a smile to his lips.

Nigel threw him off with a vicious shove. Cade landed hard on his side with his arm beneath him and heard something crack. A rib, perhaps, but he didn't have time to let the pain flood his mind. He had one goal—kill Nigel.

When the darkness shouted to be let loose, Cade threw his arms wide and his head back with his eyes closed.

"You can't beat me," Nigel howled.

Cade could feel the power building within, feel the darkness pushing free. It should have scared him. Before, he would have been trying to tamp the darkness back down. But not now.

A smile pulled at Cade's lips. The power was exhilarating as it took over. He forgot where he was, who he was. Until he opened his eyes and spotted Nigel.

Cade chuckled when Nigel took a step away from him. "Something wrong?"

Nigel shook his head. "I have more power than you."

"Maybe. Let's find out, shall we?"

"I have your witch, Cade. You should think of that before you try to harm me. With one thought, I could kill her."

Cade took a deep breath, willing the anger to fuel him. "You shouldn't have mentioned her."

"Cade. Let's talk about this."

"The time for talking is over."

Cade swirled his blades around him as he advanced on Nigel. The baron lifted his hands, palms out. Cade laughed as he rolled away from the blast of power. He came up behind Nigel.

"Your time is over."

Nigel whirled around, his eyes wide. He opened his mouth to speak, but Cade had already sliced his knives through Nigel's neck.

The baron's lips moved, but instead of words, only blood bubbled from the corners before his head tipped backwards and rolled to the ground. A heartbeat later, his body crumpled beside it.

Cade's breath came in great bursts. He smiled down at the dead body of Nigel, knowing he had succeeded in killing evil. When he turned away, Nigel's army surrounded him.

He turned back his lips in a sneer. "Who wants to join him?" he said and gestured toward Nigel.

The men looked from him to Nigel, unsure of what to do. Of a sudden, light exploded around them, knocking Cade against a tree. Pain filled his head. He struggled through a sea of nausea and throbbing as he tried to rise and find his weapons before the men attacked.

Just as his hand closed over one of his knives, he fell to the side, unconscious.

Chapter Twenty-eight

Francesca opened her eyes to find Drogan, Serena, Grayson, and Adrianna staring over her.

"Fran?" Drogan asked. "How do you feel?"

She parted her lips to speak when she remembered everything that had happened, from the torture to seeing Cade's past. It took but a moment to realize she was free.

"Where's Cade?" she asked.

Each one of them refused to meet her gaze. Dread filled her. She threw off the blanket and rose from the bed.

"Fran, please," Drina called. "You need rest."

But Francesca wasn't listening. She raced from her chamber and out of the castle. It wasn't until she was in the bailey that a large hand clamped around her arm and jerked her to a stop.

"What are you doing?" Drogan demanded.

"Cade set me free."

Drogan glanced away. "I know."

"You spoke with him?"

"Aye. He came to the castle."

Her knees threatened to buckle. "He came in the castle?"

"For you, Fran. He came for you."

Tears blurred her vision. "I don't want to lose him."

"Neither do I, but I think we have. He left to find Nigel."

Francesca glanced at the gate. "They'll be in the woods."

"I swore to Cade I would keep you safe."

There was no way to get Drogan out of the gates, and he wouldn't let her out of his sight for fear she would sneak away. "I cannot leave Cade. He's going to need me."

"Fran," Drogan began, only to halt when a knight called to him. "What is it?"

"There are men coming out of the forest, dropping their weapons."

Francesca met his gaze before they both rushed up the stairs to the battlements. With her heart pounding in her chest, she stood by Drogan and watched the men wander away from the trees.

"What does it mean?"

Drogan shrugged. "I don't know."

"Maybe Cade won."

"Nay." Drogan faced her. "He was afraid to fight Nigel, afraid that if he won, your soul wouldn't be returned. He went to give himself over to Nigel."

She gripped the stones so tightly her knuckles turned white. "You must be wrong."

An hour later, they still stood on the battlements. The men had ceased walking from the trees, and there was no more movement in the forest.

"We have to see," Francesca pleaded. "Please, Drogan. What if he's injured?"

"What if he's the monster we think he'll be?"

She lifted her chin. "Then I'll save him."

Drogan was crumbling, she could tell. She glanced at Serena, who had joined them.

"We won't know until we look," Serena said. "Take your men with you."

Drogan nodded. "Alright."

Francesca started past him, but he stopped her with a hand on her arm. "Don't think to keep me here," she threatened. "The man I love is out there, and nothing will stop me from going to him."

Drogan sighed and released her. Ten minutes later, they were atop horses, racing to the trees. Francesca didn't know what she would find, but she prayed that somehow, despite all the odds, she would make it to Cade.

They spread out through the forest, but Drogan made her stay near him. Serena, Grayson and Adrianna were also with them in case Cade needed healing.

"Over here," someone shouted.

Francesca didn't wait for Drogan. She spurred her horse toward the voice and ducked through the trees. When she pulled her horse to a halt, she found herself looking down at the headless corpse of Nigel.

"God's blood," Grayson murmured.

Francesca smiled. "Cade did it. Cade beat him."

"Then where is Cade?" Drogan asked.

She slid from her horse. A moment later, Drogan and Grayson did the same, each cursing beneath their breaths. She didn't care, though. All that mattered was Cade.

It wasn't until she rounded a tree that she saw him. He was lying on his side, blood oozing from a cut on his forehead. Her blood froze in her veins as she knelt beside him. She put her hand over his heart and felt it beating.

"He's alive," she said between her tears.

She turned him onto his back, and he groaned.

"Step back, Fran," Drogan warned. "You don't know what Cade will be when he opens his eyes."

And she didn't care. Cade was hers. She leaned down and placed her lips on his. His eyes fluttered and opened, showing blue irises instead of red.

She lifted her head and smoothed her hand down his face. "I thought I'd lost you."

"Francesca?"

She closed her eyes for a heartbeat and smiled. "That's the first time you've called me by my name."

"I've done it a million times in my mind."

"Are you hurt?"

"Nothing that can't be cured by your presence."

"Cade, I—" she began, but he stopped her with a finger over her lips.

His face hardened. "I know what Nigel showed you. You don't need to pretend to care for me."

Her heart tore in two at the sound of resignation in his voice. "Do you think my love so shallow that I couldn't see your pain? That I couldn't tell how it nearly killed you not to be able to fight the darkness? That I couldn't feel your agony as clearly as my own?"

Hope leapt into his eyes, and more tears fell down her cheeks. "Regardless of the darkness inside you, I love you, Cade."

His face twisted with anguish. "You can't mean that. I don't deserve it."

Francesca kissed him again and put her forehead to his. "You deserve love most of all."

For a moment, he didn't move. Then his arms came around her and he crushed his mouth to hers, kissing her as if there were no tomorrow. The kiss was frantic and full of love and lust.

Francesca groaned when he ended the kiss.

Cade looked into the clear, tawny gaze of his witch. She loved him, despite everything. She really loved him. It was there in her eyes, in her touch, for all to see. He'd never been more humbled in his life.

"I love you." He finally said the words, knowing he had loved her since that first kiss.

She laughed, the sound heavenly and perfect.

"I'd like to leave the two of you alone, but Cade, you're injured," Drogan said, his voice amused.

Cade looked up to find it wasn't just Drogan, Serena, Grayson and Adrianna watching them, but the fifty knights Drogan had brought as well.

Francesca moved off him, and with the help of Drogan and Grayson, Cade got to his feet. He winced when he tried to take a breath.

"What happened to your head?" Drina asked as she came towards him.

Cade shrugged and watched Drogan send his men back to the castle. "I remember killing Nigel and facing his men, and then there was this light. I was thrown back, and I don't remember much after that."

"You really killed him," Francesca said. "I was supposed to do that."

He frowned. "You nearly got yourself killed."

"I'd seen it every night in my visions, Cade. I had beaten him every time."

"Then what did he say to make you hesitate?" Serena asked.

Francesca smiled as she looked at him. "He threatened Cade. I knew he would, and I thought I could withstand anything he said. But I was wrong."

Cade pushed Drina's hands from his own and pulled Francesca into his arms. "Don't ever risk your life like that again."

"Of course I will if you or someone else I love is in danger and I can save them."

He didn't know how he had managed to live his life without her, but he knew he couldn't continue another moment alone.

"What?" she whispered. "What is it?"

"I never thought to love someone like this."

She smiled and cupped his face. "Me either."

"I know I'm not worthy of you, but I want you. Forever, witch."

"Then I am yours. Forever."

"And the curse?"

She shrugged. "I survived Nigel. Besides, if Grayson's parents, Serena and Adrianna can break the curse, so can I."

"*We* can break the curse," he said.

"Aye, we can break the curse."

He kissed her again, long and slow. "Will you marry me?"

"Aye, my lord. I will marry you."

Epilogue

Four months later

Cade stood with Francesca as they looked at Stonelake, the home he had thought never to see again.

"It's beautiful, Cade. Simply stunning."

He smiled at her and wrapped his arm around his wife. They hadn't hesitated to get married. The darkness had left him just as all the souls had returned to their owners upon Nigel's death.

Cade wasn't sure how, nor did he care. He was just glad to have the darkness gone and once more be himself. He had wanted to return home sooner, but he had spent some time with Drogan. That also gave his steward time to get things ready for their arrival at Stonelake.

Now that he was here, though, he wasn't sure he could go inside.

"It'll be all right," Francesca said.

Cade wasn't so sure. Maybe the ghosts of his family waited to torture him.

"They knew it wasn't you that day, Cade. They knew."

He entwined his fingers with hers and smiled. They nudged their horses into a walk, and he couldn't help but glance at Francesca's rounding stomach. She was almost four months along. To know he had found love, a wife, and was returning home to raise his child seemed surreal. Francesca had given him hope, a hope that had consumed him.

Dreams of his future once more filled his mind. He had his home and lands and a brave, beautiful woman by his side. He would have to earn the trust of his people, but he had no doubt with Francesca beside him, he would accomplish even that.

As for the curse that had haunted Francesca's people, it no longer held sway over her. Just as he had told her, the curse was only as powerful as people let it be.

"Are you ready?" she whispered as they neared the gatehouse where guards stared down at him.

Inside the bailey, he could hear people shouting that he had returned, and it wasn't fear he heard in their voices. It was hope.

He tugged on Francesca's arm until she leaned over so he could kiss her. "I'm ready."

"Then let us face our future."

"Together."

She smiled as they rode under the gatehouse. "Together."

SHADOW MAGIC

The first book of the *Sisters of Magic* trilogy

With a past soaked in sin and darkness slowly closing in around him to claim his soul, Drogan only wants to live his life in solitude. Years in the king's service and his numerous deeds directed by the crown have left Drogan with horrendous nightmares and immeasurable guilt...

Serena is a witch, cursed and forever alone. She accepts her future. Until she meets Drogan. With Drogan a passion deep and unyielding awakens inside her. She is willing to sacrifice herself for his love, but can he put his past to rest and embrace the future?

ECHOES OF MAGIC

The second book in the *Sisters of Magic* trilogy

Hiding a secret so awful that his only hope for survival is to remain hidden, Grayson has lived most of his life pretending to be someone he isn't. After years serving as a commander to his lord and friend, Grayson can no longer hold back the past. He leaves in search of answers only to find evil awaits him. Until he discovers an achingly beautiful woman who stirs his deepest passions and all consuming need.

Adrianna knows what her future holds for her as a witch - loneliness and heartache. She has accepted that. Until she discovers Grayson near death in the forest. Saving him is her only choice, and even as she falls deeper into the attraction surrounding them, can her magic be enough to stop Fate or the evil that awaits them.

Read on for an excerpt from

A DARK GUARDIAN

the first in the thrilling
Shield series

The darkness of night summoned Evil like a warm tavern to a weary traveler. The velvety thickness blanketed any who dared to oppose its will. And the Evil enfolding Stone Crest had one task in mind - the demise of all.

"Faster," Mina whispered urgently into her mare's ear. She bent low over the horse's neck and chanced a look over her shoulder, her hair sticking to her face and neck as the ground raced beneath her.

The dark, menacing road was vacant, but she knew the creature was near. Stalking. Mina's skin tingled with anticipation, and her heart pounded fiercely in her chest as her mare continued to run toward the trees.

A terrible, unearthly scream rent the air. Mina quickly covered her ears. Her mare slowed, then stopped and danced around in fright.

"Nay," Mina hissed while she tried to gain control of her mount. "Run, Sasha, run. Our lives depend upon it."

The mare sensed Mina's anxiety because her long legs stretched out and the ground flew beneath them once more. Mina gripped the reins and Sasha's mane tightly as her blood rushed wildly with fear and dread. The hair on the back of her neck rose, but she didn't need to look behind her to know the creature followed very close.

Mina focused on reaching the clearing. Her mare was fleet of foot, the swiftest of her family's horses. If anyone could outrun the creature, it was Sasha. At least, Mina had thought so. Now she wasn't so sure.

A small smile formed on her face when she saw the clump of trees that signaled the clearing was just a short distance away. As she was about to reach the trees, the flap of wings overhead reached her.

Something long and sharp passed in front of her face and sliced across her arm. A frantic Sasha reared, and it was all Mina could do to hang on. Then suddenly, the world tilted and Mina jumped clear as her beloved mare collapsed and lay too still on her side.

Mina raised her eyes to the night sky and saw the creature that had come to their small village hovering above her, a sardonic smile on its grotesque face. Its small beady eyes flashed red in the gloom, and she knew her time was at an end.

Long, razor-sharp talons lengthened from its hands. She swallowed her failure like a lump of coal. This wasn't how it was supposed to end.

Fear immobilized her. She couldn't even scream. The creature moved slowly in the air towards her, as if he wanted to torment her prior to killing her. Before the creature's talons carved open her face, she saw a blur of movement out of the corner of her eye. In the next moment, she found herself thrown roughly to the ground and over the side of the hill. The weight of whoever had landed atop her knocked the wind from her lungs in a gush. As they rolled, she dimly heard the furious screams of the creature.

Just as she thought they might tumble for eternity, they finally came to an abrupt, bone-jarring halt. She was afraid to open her eyes and find that another evil had taken her. After all, it had been the worst kind of wickedness, which had plagued her village for a month now.

A deep, soft voice reached her ears through her panic. A man's voice. "Are you all right?"

Slowly, she opened her eyes. Instead of a face, all she saw was the outline of his head. His tone held a hint of concern, but this was a stranger. She had come to mistrust anything that wasn't part of her village.

"Aye," she answered at last.

"I was beginning to think the fall had addled your brain." There was no mistaking the trace of humor in his meaning as he swiftly rose to his feet.

He held out a hand to her. She hated to do it, but she accepted his help because she didn't think she could gain her feet alone after the tumble she had just taken. As he pulled her to her feet, her arm burst into agonizing pain. She could barely move her hand, but she wasn't about to let the stranger know she was hurt and give him an advantage. It was something she had learned early in life. One had to be strong to survive in this land.

"It's not a safe night for a woman to be out alone."

She sensed he wanted to say more but held back. They were mere inches from each other, so she took a step back to offer herself more room. "There are many things which should keep people safely inside at night. Including men."

He bowed his head slightly. "I mean you no harm, lady."

She didn't believe that for an instant. Only a wandering idiot would take a stranger's word.

A bizarre whistle-like noise sounded from atop the hill. The stranger whistled back and then the eerie silence reigned once more. Not even the sound of crickets could be heard.

With her good hand she dusted off her breeches, and looked around for the dagger she had swiped from the armory. She couldn't believe she had dropped her only weapon.

"Is this what you seek?"

Mina grudgingly turned to the man and saw her dagger in his outstretched hand. She accepted the weapon. "Thank you. For everything." She bit her lip and thought of Sasha. Without another word, she began to race up the hill.

The stranger was at her side in an instant, aiding her when she would have fallen. When they reached the top, she came to a halt as five men on horseback stared at her. They sat atop their steeds like kings, watching her every move. She dismissed them when Sasha's soft cry of pain reached her.

She went to her mare and knelt beside her. She ran her hand lightly over the open gash across Sasha's whither and closed her eyes. It was a mortal wound.

"The mare has lost a lot of blood," the stranger said as he knelt beside Sasha. "I'm afraid she is lost to you."

Tears came quickly to Mina's eyes, and she tried to blink them away. Tears were for the weak. "I'm so sorry, Sasha," she said and leaned down to kiss the mare's head. "I should never have come."

She knew there was no way to save her horse, and to leave her like this was to see her suffer needlessly. With trembling hands, she held the dagger to Sasha's throat, but moments slowly drew on.

A large, warm hand encased hers. "Shall I?" the stranger offered.

Before she could change her mind she nodded. He took the dagger and she laid her head on Sasha's. It was over in a heartbeat. Sasha never made a sound, but it cut through Mina's soul like a silent scream of anguish.

She gave herself but a moment before she stood and looked around her as the moon broke through the dense clouds. Now she was alone with six men. Six heavily armed strangers.

The stranger rose and faced her. "I am Hugh."

"From where do you come?"

"London," he answered after a bit of a hesitation. He extended his arm to the men on horseback. "My companions are Roderick, Val, Gabriel, Cole and Darrick."

Each man bowed his head as Hugh said his name, and she was quick to note the array of weapons and the large shields, even in the cloud-laden night. Then, six pairs of eyes were on her.

"I am Lady Mina of Stone Crest."

"Well, Lady Mina, what manner of men would allow you to be out at night unprotected?"

Hugh's question had her thinking of the trap she and some of the villagers had set. "I'm not alone," she said with more conviction than she felt. Her eyes scanned the sky above her, but there was no sign of the creature.

"Where are your men?"

She turned and pointed toward the clump of trees. "In the clearing. I was luring a...an animal into a trap."

When she turned toward the men, the moonlight lit upon Hugh for just an instant, but in that moment she saw his skepticism. "It would have worked," she defended herself. "If Sasha had made it to the clearing."

"I hate to point out the obvious," the man in the middle said. Gabriel was his name. "But your men have yet to come to your aid."

Fear snaked its way through her and nestled comfortably in her stomach. These men could easily kill her. "I have only to call to them."

"Then call for I would meet the manner of men who would allow a woman to take such a risk," Hugh stated, his voice laden with unspoken anger.

"I would rather see the trap," Gabriel said and nudged his horse forward.

She stood her ground, ready to bolt, as Gabriel and his mount walked past her. She nearly sighed aloud, but recalled that she wasn't alone.

Hugh watched Mina closely. Her hesitation said all he needed to know. The men that should have been with her had deserted her. Had she lied? Was she alone?

The creature she had lured must have frightened them away. Yet, if what she said was indeed true and they had set a trap, then the men wouldn't have deserted her.

"Come," he said and put his hand on her back to guide her toward the clearing.

She walked a little ahead of him, and he tried not to notice that she wore breeches instead of a gown. It had been awhile since he had given in to his urges and bedded a woman, and with one walking just ahead of him with her backside swaying so enticingly from side to side, he found it hard to ignore.

He mentally shook himself and made his eyes look away from her delectable back end. Her hair had come loose from her braid and hung down her back in thick waves. Its exact color was hard to detect in the darkness, but he knew it was pale.

Thankfully, they reached the clearing then. Just as he suspected, no one waited for her. "Where is the trap?" he asked.

"I was to lead the creature into those trees," she said and pointed straight ahead. "Once I passed them, the men would cut a rope that held a spike which would impale the...animal."

Hugh heard the hesitation and wondered when she would tell them exactly what manner of beast had been chasing her. Could it be she really didn't know? Despite his misgivings about the situation, they had been sent to help.

And an order was an order

The creak of leather sounded loudly in the quiet as someone dismounted, and when Hugh looked over he found Gabriel beside him.

"Not a bad plan," Gabriel said thoughtfully as he stared at the trees. "I wonder if it would have worked."

"I guess we'll never know," Mina said softly.

"Scout the area," Hugh told his men. "See if any of Lady Mina's men are still around."

While his men did as ordered he handed Mina his water skin. She drank greedily before returning it to him.

"We aren't here to harm you."

She shrugged her shoulder. "We've learned not to trust anyone. Are you knights?"

"In a manner," he answered. "Do your parents know what you were about tonight?"

"They are dead."

That explained much. "By the beast that was after you?"

She became very still before she briefly nodded her head. "You know what hunts us?"

"I do," he admitted.

"How?" Her voice held doubt and hope.

"I'll explain once you're safe. Do you have any other family?"

"A brother and sister, and they did know what I was doing," she answered before he could ask.

Before Hugh could ask more questions, his men returned without good news. It was just as he expected, and it left a foul taste in mouth. There was no excuse to leave a defenseless woman alone to face the sort of evil they hunted.

"We will return you home safely." When she hesitated he said, "If you would prefer to face that creature alone and on foot, then we will leave you to it."

He had an idea she was about to do just that when the creature screamed some distance away and silenced any words she might have said. Without waiting for her to agree, he swiftly lifted her onto his horse.

He glanced at his men before he grabbed his horse's reins and mounted behind her. Their expressions said it all.

They had found exactly what they searched for.

Author Bio

Bestselling, award-winning author Donna Grant has been praised for her "totally addictive" and "unique and sensual" stories. She's the author of more than twenty novels spanning multiple genres of romance--Scottish Medieval, dark fantasy, time travel, paranormal, and erotic. Her latest acclaimed series, Dark Sword, features a thrilling combination of Druids, primeval gods, and immortal Highlanders who are dark, dangerous, and irresistible. She lives with her husband, two children, a dog, and three cats in Texas.

Visit Donna at www.DonnaGrant.com

2386157R00112

Printed in Great Britain
by Amazon.co.uk, Ltd.,
Marston Gate.